GOOD 2 GO

# The Teflon Queen 4
## MR. DEATH

A Novel

## SILK WHITE

Good2Go Publishing

ISBN: 9780990869429

Copyright ©2015 by Silk White

Published 2015 by Good2Go Publishing

7311 W. Glass Lane • Laveen, AZ 85339

www.good2gopublishing.com

twitter @good2gobooks

G2G@good2gopublishing.com

Facebook.com/good2gopublishing

ThirdLane Marketing: Brian James

Brian@good2gopublishing.com

Editor: Kesha Buckhana

Cover design: Davida Baldwin

# Books by This Author

*Married To Da Streets*

*Never Be The Same*

*Stranded*

*Tears of a Hustler*

*Tears of a Hustler 2*

*Tears of a Hustler 3*

*Tears of a Hustler 4*

*Tears of a Hustler 5*

*Tears of a Hustler 6*

*Teflon Queen*

*Teflon Queen 2*

*Teflon Queen 3*

*Teflon Queen 4*

*Time Is Money (An Anthony Stone Novel)*

*48 Hours to Die (An Anthony Stone Novel)*

## Acknowledgments

To all of you who are reading this, thank you for stepping inside the bookstore, stopping by the library, or downloading a copy of The Teflon Queen 4. I hope you have enjoyed this read from top to bottom. My goal is to get better and better with each story. I want to thank everyone for all their love and support. It is definitely appreciated! Now without further ado Ladies and Gentleman, I give you *The Teflon Queen 4*. Enjoy!

# PROLOGUE

Ashley sat behind the wheel of an all-black Dodge Charger. She'd been tailing a limousine for the past hour. Her target was a middle-aged man that resided in the back of the limousine. Her mission was to terminate the man, retrieve the suitcase he possessed, and return it to her boss. For the past four years, Ashley had been working for the Central Intelligence Agency (CIA) and had become one of their best agents. She used all the skills that Angela had taught her years ago and perfected them, she now used those same skills to capture and kill terrorist. Ashley's target was a man that went by the name, Muhammad Ockbar. He was one of the most deadly terrorist to ever walk the earth. His sole purpose for living was to destroy America and become filthy rich in the process. Ashley couldn't even count on her fingers and toes combined how many Americans that Muhammad had killed in the past six months.

"Muhammad's hotel is coming up on your right a few blocks away on your left," a voice chirped inside Ashley's ear piece.

"Copy," she replied. It was close to show time and the butterflies in her stomach were doing summersaults. Ashley stepped out of the Charger dressed in a black tight fitting dress that left little to the imagination. Her face was freshly done in a nice coat of makeup and a long straight haired black wig gave her a more exotic look. Ashley stepped out the car, handed the valley her keys and entered the hotel.

"You are going to have about a four-minute window to get this done," the voice in her ear piece informed her.

"I'll only need two Troy," Ashley said as she took hurried steps and stuck her hand in the elevator just as the doors were about to close. "Sorry," she smiled as she piled on the elevator along with Muhammad and his team of security. "Can you press twelve for me, please?"

8

The bodyguard pressed twelve eyeing Ashley suspiciously.

He figured her to be a high priced prostitute, but just to be on the safe side his hand quickly dropped down to his waistline.

The ride on the elevator was a quiet one. Ashley glanced over at Muhammad and noticed a briefcase handcuffed to his wrist. Whatever was inside that briefcase was worth his right hand. The elevator reached the twelfth floor and immediately Ashley stepped off and headed down the hall, followed by Muhammad and his team.

Ashley could feel all eyes on her with each step she took. She entered her room that was right next door to Muhammad's room by design. Once inside the room Ashley quickly walked over to the bed that had a duffle bag sitting on top. She reached inside and removed a stick of C-4 and stuck in on the wall, she then walked back over to the duffle bag, removed a P89, and screwed a silencer on the barrel.

"Two minutes, Muhammad's second team of security just pulled up in front of the hotel," Troy's voice sounded off in her ear piece.

Ashley quickly grabbed the remote from out of the duffle

bag, pressed the red button, and the C-4 immediately exploded blowing a huge hole in the wall. Once the explosion was over, Ashley quickly walked through the wall and into Muhammad's room. The first thing she saw was Muhammad's security coughing from all the smoke. Ashley raised her gun, fired three shots in rapid succession and three security guards were down. The last guard grabbed Ashley from behind in a bear hug. Ashley smoothly fired a shot into his shoe causing him to release his grip, she then quickly spun around and pumped three shots into the man's chest and watched him crumble down to the floor. Ashley then turned her attention to Muhammad. He held the briefcase close to his chest as if it were a new born baby.

"You're making a big mistake!" He barked.

Without warning, Ashley put a bullet between Muhammad's eyes, then turned and shot his right hand off and removed the briefcase. She quickly made a bee line for the door. "What am I'm looking like?" She asked taking hurried steps towards the elevator.

"A team of eight are coming your way, four on the elevator, four in the staircase pick your poison," Troy replied.

"Think, think, think," Ashley said to herself. She had to make a split decision and time wasn't on her side. The bell sounded notifying that the elevator had arrived. Just as the four men stepped off the elevator, Ashley smoothly slid in staircase unseen. Knowing more than likely she would wind up having to get busy, Ashley removed her heels and proceeded down the stairs barefoot.

As Ashley made her way down the stairs, she could hear the sound of multiple footsteps coming up the steps. She quickly held her P89 behind her thigh. The first man had a rough face with a huge nasty looking beard covering his face. Ashley walked past the first guy but noticed the second guy eyeing the briefcase she was carrying. Without hesitation, Ashley swung the briefcase with all her might breaking the man's nose instantly. She then spun around and shot the first gunman in the throat. The third gunman froze as a deer caught in the headlights. Seconds later, his brains popped out the back of his skull and painted the wall red. Ashley aimed her gun at the last gunman and pulled the trigger.

"Click!"

The gunman slapped the empty gun out of Ashley's hand, locked his hand around her throat, and forcefully rushed her back to the wall. Ashley raised her foot and kicked the gunman's knee cap in the opposite direction. The sound of his bone snapping sounded off loudly throughout the staircase. Ashley grabbed the back of the gunman's head and delivered a crushing knee to his face. She then held the gunman's head in a firm grip and twisted it with force in the opposite direction until she heard it snap. Ashley picked the briefcase up off the floor and proceeded down to the lobby of the hotel.

"Are you okay?" Troy asked.

"On my way out now," Ashley replied as she reached the lobby. She quickly blended in with the crowd and took hurried steps towards the exit. As soon as Ashley, stepped foot out of the hotel, a black van pulled up and she quickly hopped in the back. She wasn't even all the way inside the van before it pulled off into traffic.

"Good work back there," Troy said with a smile.

"Don't mention it," Ashley returned his smile, then handed him the briefcase.

Troy quickly pulled out a device and placed it on top of the briefcase just to make sure that whatever was inside wouldn't explode. Once he was sure it wouldn't explode, he proceeded to crack the code to the suitcase.

Troy opened the briefcase and the first thing he noticed was a black bag made out of cloth. He smiled as he opened the bag and found that it was filled with diamonds. Also inside the briefcase, was some sort of a blueprint. After further observation, Troy realized that the blueprint was to a building out in New York City. Troy looked over at Ashley and smiled. "I think you just stopped a major bombing,"

Ashley smiled. Things like this made the job worth all the risk. Ever since meeting Angela years ago, Ashley had been obsessed with the assassin's lifestyle. It was said around headquarters that Ashley was the best agent they had ever seen and that was all thanks to Angela and her training.

"You're sure to get a medal for this one," Troy raised his hand for a high five. Troy had been Ashley's partner ever since she joined the force.

"Of course I couldn't of had done this without you," Ashley

said honestly. "But this is just a small piece to the puzzle. Now that we've gotten Abdul's son out of the picture he's sure to retaliate.

Abdul Ockbar was known as the world's most vicious and most wanted terrorist since Osama Bin Laden. He was known for bombing other countries, extortion, and he had an army of trained killers that were willing to die for Abdul, their country, and the cause.

"Maybe this may bring that scumbag out of hiding," Troy said.

Ashley reached headquarters and headed straight to her Lieutenant's office. Lieutenant Banks sat behind his desk with an angry look on his face which wasn't out of the ordinary. Even when he was happy, he still had a scowl on his face. "Hope you have some good news for me," his voice boomed.

Ashley smiled and sat the bag of diamonds down on his desk along with the blueprint to the New York building. "Muhammad is dead; next up his father Abdul."

"You killed Muhammad?" Lieutenant Banks asked cracking a smile for once. "It's about time causing I'm sick of these

14

terrorists fucks always trying to blow something up," he shook his head. "Maybe this may bring Abdul out of hiding," he said with a raised brow.

"Hopefully," Ashley replied.

"Good work Ashley," Lieutenant Banks stood and shook Ashley's hand. "Go home and get you some rest and I'll call you tomorrow."

"Thank you sir," Ashley said and then made her exit.

Once Lieutenant Banks was sure that Ashley was gone, he picked up his phone and dialed a number. It rung four times before a man with a scratchy voice answer. "Hello?"

"Hey Abdul; it's Banks."

"I know who it is the question is what do you want?" Abdul said in an irritated tone.

"I'm afraid I have some bad news for you," Lieutenant Banks paused for a second. He had been doing business with the world's biggest terrorist for the past three years and had no complaints. "Your son Muhammad was murdered today."

Abdul was silent for a second. "And what about my diamonds?"

"I got the diamonds back, but that building you were planning to take down in New York you're going to have to cancel that the blueprint was discovered."

"You assured me that I wouldn't have any problems from your people," Abdul barked. "What the fuck am I paying you for?"

"Sorry about that, there was just a slight mix up on my end and I can assure you something like this won't happen again," Lieutenant Banks promised. His biggest fear was getting cut off. He'd never made as much money as he was now until he started doing business with Abdul.

"Who killed my son?" Abdul asked in a deadly tone.

"Special Agent Ashley Brown, but no need to worry I'll take care of her tonight." Lieutenant Banks said.

"I have a few men in your area right now," Abdul said. "My men will take care of this problem just lead them in the right direction."

"No disrespect but are your men any good?" Lieutenant Banks asked. "Agent Ashley is no joke."

"My men are well trained and are more than capable to take

out one female," said Abdul. "You just make sure something like this never happens again or else!"

"You got my word something like this will never happen again."

"One of my men will call you in the next five minutes for Agent Brown's address and whereabouts," Abdul said and ended the call not allowing Lieutenant Banks a chance to respond.

# CHAPTER | 1 MR. DEATH

Ashley eased her way down into the bathtub. The water was smoking hot but it was just how Ashley liked it. She lived in a small town house in the middle of nowhere, she chose to be isolated, and away from others, something she had learned from her mentor Angela. Ashley didn't want to have to deal with neighbors. She enjoyed the quietness and her privacy.

Ashley and her team had been after Muhammad for months and to finally take him out was a breath of fresh air. She knew that this was just the beginning and expected some form of retaliation to come once the word about Muhammad's death got out there. Ashley sipped on a glass of red wine and grabbed the letter that she had received from Angela off the toilet seat. Ashley and Angela made sure they stayed in contact. They wrote each other letters at least once a week. Ashley sipped from her glass and began reading the letter.

Hey Ashley how's it going out there? I've been good just watching CNN. I've been hearing about these bomb threats going on and I just wanted to say please be careful out there. I never wanted this for you, but you are grown and all I can do is try and give you advice. I received the money you sent me; I told you that you don't have to keep sending me money I'm all right. Be careful and keep your eyes open out there and if you ever need me I'll be there for you. Love always your big sis the Teflon Queen.

After reading the letter, all Ashley could do was smile. She couldn't express the amount of love that she had for Angela and how much she appreciated her for saving her life years ago. Sometimes she wondered where she would be or what she would be doing if it weren't for Angela. Ashley took another sip of wine when she heard her cell phone ring. She looked at the screen and saw Troy's name flashing across the screen. "Hey Troy what's up?" She answered.

"Work, work, and more work," Troy said with stress all in his tone. He loved being a special agent but sometimes he felt like the job was beginning to take over his life. "Just got word that Abdul is sending one of his best hit men to the states to retrieve the diamonds that we stole today."

"Lieutenant Banks know about this?"

"Yes he's having the diamonds moved to a safe location now," Troy said.

"Who's the hit man?"

"Some guy named Mr. Death," Troy replied. "He's a Japanese hit man slash ninja and from what I hear he's supposed to be the real deal."

"I think I heard of him before," Ashley replied. She had heard stories about how violent and deadly the assassin was. If he was on his way to the states trouble was sure to follow. "Do me a favor get me all the information you can on this Mr. Death guy and get back to me tomorrow," Ashley went to say something else when all of a sudden the lights in the entire house went out. "My lights just went out."

"Did the bulb blow?" Troy asked.

Ashley paused and listened. The sound of someone fumbling around with the locks on the front door could be heard followed by the sound of glass shattering. "I've got company. I gotta go."

"I'm on my way!" Troy said ending the call.

Ashley quickly stepped out of the tub and grabbed her Five-seven pistol with the silencer screwed onto the barrel that rested on the edge of the sink. It may have been dark but Ashley knew her away around her house so having no lights wouldn't be a problem for her. Ashley was about to run to her closet and grab something to put on real quick, but the sound of footsteps coming up the steps forced her to stay put. The first man around the corner was rewarded with a bullet to the head. Ashley surprised the next gunman and delivered a blow to the man's temple with the butt of her gun. The blow knocked the gunman unconscious, Ashley caught his body before it hit the floor and used him as a human shield. Immediately the sound of gun fire erupted throughout the house. Ashley could feel the impact from the

21

bullets ripping through the gunman she used as a shield body. Ashley was quickly able to see where the gun men were positioned from the fire that flashed from the muzzle of their weapons. She fired off three shots, pushed the dead gunman down the steps, and then took cover behind the wall closes to her. Ashley was sure that the three shots she fired found homes in her intended targets the only problem was she had no idea how many gunmen had showed up to her home. As Ashley stood behind the wall, several infrared beams dotted the wall next to her in search of a target. The next brave gunmen ran upstairs and immediately two shots to the face sent him right back down the steps. Ashley stood in her position and noticed more and more infrared beams dot the walls. Her main concern was keeping the gunmen downstairs until Troy and her back up arrived.

Ashley was just about to make a move when one of the gunmen tossed a grenade upstairs. "Shit!" She cursed as she took off into a full sprint down the hall. She had only made it a few steps when the force from the explosion violently tossed her body into the bedroom.

The lead gunman led his troops up the steps. The heat from

22

the explosion had sweat trickling down the side of his face. When he and his men had been assigned to kill a woman he was expecting it to be like taking candy from a baby, but instead it was turning out to be more difficult than he ever would of imagined. He made it upstairs and inched his way down the hall, not knowing what to expect. He stepped further into the room and suddenly his feet were swept from under him and a knife was jammed down into his throat before he even knew what happened. Three gunmen entered the bedroom next and opened fire. They didn't have an eye on the target but opened fire anyway hoping to maybe him their target with a lucky shot. Once the gunfire ceased the gunman noticed, the man right next to him drop down to the floor. He then felt a bullet rip through his stomach. The impact from the shot forced him to drop down to his knees. A bullet to the side of the head then silenced him forever. The next gunman entered the bedroom with a look of fear on his face. He could barely see in the dark not to mention there were only two other gunmen still breathing. He walked slowly through the bedroom when he heard a sound coming from his right. He quickly spun to his right and squeezed down on the trigger of his machine. His bullets tore through the wall leaving a raggedy design in the wall. Once he was sure that no one was there, he breathed a sigh of relief. He took another step forward when a wire was suddenly wrapped around his neck, the gunman dropped his weapon as his hands instantly tried to grip the wire but it was no use the wire was already too deep into his skin for him to stop what was destined to happen. The next gunman stepped foot in the bedroom and stopped when he saw something shiny coming at him in rapid speed. A throwing knife found a home in the center of his throat. The last gunman stepped in the bedroom and squeezed down on the trigger of his gun swaying his arms back and forth. He quickly reloaded and squeezed down on the trigger again. Once his magazine was empty, he went to reload again, but paused when he heard a noise coming from behind him. The gunman spun around and saw a dark figure coming at him full speed. She leaped through the air and landed a flying kick to the gunman's chest that sent him crashing dramatically through the bedroom's window.

Ashley looked out the window at the gunman's body and smiled at her handy work. She was just about to go downstairs when she saw Troy's car come to a screeching halt in front of her house. He quickly hopped out the car with an assault rifle in his hands and ran towards the front door. Ashley met Troy at the top of the steps. "I handle it already,"

"You okay?" Troy asked noticing that Ashley's naked body was covered in blood in certain spots.

"It's not my blood," Ashley said quickly. She was comfortable with her nakedness around people so the fact that she was naked in front of Troy didn't bother her. "You heard from Lieutenant Banks?"

"Yes he wants to see us immediately," Troy said.

Ashley took a quick shower, cleaned off, got dress, then her and Troy were out the door.

# CHAPTER

## 2 TAKE IT OR LEAVE IT

Ashley and Troy reached headquarters and headed straight for Lieutenant Banks office.

"What happened?" Lieutenant Banks barked.

"A mob of shooters broke into my house and tried to kill me!" Ashley shouted. "They have someone working on the inside!"

"Don't be ridiculous!" Lieutenant Banks countered.

"There is no way they would have found out where I live, no way!" Ashley fumed. "There's a mole in here somewhere!"

"Listen let's not jump to conclusions," Lieutenant Banks said. "If there is a mole, we'll get to the bottom of it."

"In this business I have to be able to trust and right now I have no trust until I find out how they found out where I live," Ashley stated plainly. "I have a bull's-eye on my back right now and the bounty is probably a ridiculous amount. I need someone that I can trust to watch my back.

"So is there anybody that you feel that you can trust?" Lieutenant Banks asked with a raised brow.

"The only person I can trust is my mentor," Ashley said.

"No way! She's a murderer!" Lieutenant Banks barked. "She's in prison where she belongs!"

"She's is prison for saving my life!" Ashley corrected him. "If anyone can make this happen, it's you Lieutenant," she paused. "I need her right now."

"You may be asking for too much this time Ashley," Lieutenant Banks said. In all reality, he was hoping that Abdul's hit squad had killed Ashley so the heat would be off of him, now that she was still alive only made matters even worst.

"I killed Abdul's son, you know he's not going to stop until I'm six feet in the ground!"

"We'll figure something out."

"What about Mr. Death?" Ashley asked.

"Word is he's on his way to the states now," Lieutenant Banks said with a worried look on his face. He knew that if he didn't deliver the diamonds to Abdul that he too would soon be on Mr. Death's hit list and that's the last thing he wanted. "He's known to be the deadliest assassin to ever walk the earth," Lieutenant Banks paused. "The word is he's been trained since birth to be a killing machine, he's just as deadly with his hands and feet as he is with any weapon."

"We know we've done our research on him," Troy said speaking for the first time. "In the files it says that he's immune to pain."

"I say we go after him before he has time to get settled and set up his attack," Ashley suggested. She wasn't into waiting around for someone to kill her.

"That's insane," Lieutenant Banks snapped. "Ashley you need to relax and let me handle this."

"Abdul is up to something big I can feel it," Troy said. "Ashley may be right we may need to attack him first instead of waiting around to be attacked."

"Troy if I want your opinion I'll give it to you!" Lieutenant Banks snapped. "Now if y'all are done telling me how to do my job maybe I'll be able to get some work done."

Ashley said. "I need the Teflon Queen."

"I'll see what I can do," Lieutenant Banks said.

"No make it happen."

* * *

After talking to Lieutenant Banks and getting nowhere, Ashley decided to go over his head and speak directly to the Captain. Captain Spiller was very strict to say the least, but when he came to getting things done, he was the man to see. Ashley and Troy entered Captain's Spiller's office and she got straight to the point. "Hey Captain I'm here to ask a big favor," Ashley began. "I know you are not a big fan of breaking rules, but I believe for this situation we may not have no choice,"

"Get to the point Ashley!" Captain Spiller barked nodding down to all the paperwork that sat scattered across his desk.

"I think we may have a mold in the unit sir."

"And you think that because?"

"I killed Abdul's son the other day and that same night a team of professional killers showed up at my home," Ashley said. "Now I hear that Abdul is up to something real big and sent an assassin named Mr. Death to the states."

Captain Spiller immediately crumbled when the name Mr.

Death was mentioned. "Mr. Death has killed over one hundred of my agents," he said with a sour taste in his mouth.

"Sir I think instead of sitting around waiting to be attacked I say we going after Mr. Death and Abdul and bring those scum bags down, but in order for me to pull this off I'm going to need some help."

"Name it."

"Sir I need the Teflon Queen," Ashley said. "And before you say anything sir she's the only one that will be able to help me take these two men down, not to mention she's the only person I trust."

"Absolutely not!" Captain Spiller's voice boomed. "Angela is a loose cannon! It took us years to finally catch her!"

"Captain," Ashley began. "You have to admit that Angela is great at what she does, but just imagine all the good she could do if she was on our side," she pointed out.

"The answer is no there's no way you'll be able to control her," Captain Spiller pinched the bridge of his nose. What Ashley was saying made sense but if anything went wrong he would be the one in the fire not Ashley, and honestly, it was just too risky for his likings. "What happens if this Teflon Queen woman gets out and goes on another killing spree then what? Can you assure me that you can control her?"

"Yes I can."

"How?"

"I give you my word if she gets out and goes against us I'll personally put her down myself," Ashley said in a stern tone letting Captain Spiller known that she was dead serious.

Captain Spiller sat quiet for a moment in his own thoughts. He had a lot to lose if this thing blew up in his face, but on the flip side if Ashley and Angela could deliver as she said they could he would look like a genius. Decisions. "I'm going to give you a shot agent Brown, but if this shit blows up in my face I'm going to have your ass! Understood?"

"Understood," Ashley smiled. Not only was she pulling strings to get her mentor and friend out of jail but she was also giving Angela a chance to do some good in her life. "I promise I won't let you down Captain."

"I'll start working on the paperwork now," he said with an uncertain look on his face. Captain Spiller had no idea how this thing was going to play out but what he did know was that if he didn't do something that plenty more of his agents would turn up dead once Mr. Death made it to the states.

Ashley got up and headed for the door, but stopped when Captain Spiller called out to her.

"Agent Brown I sure hope you know what you're doing."

"Me too."

# CHAPTER | 3 SURPRISE, SURPRISE

A ngela sat in her cell reading a good book. For the past eight years, Angela decided to improve her vocabulary and gain as much knowledge as she could. She was now used to and okay with the fact that she would be spending the rest of her life in jail. With her being in jail for so long she had time to reflect and think back on all the things that she'd done and accomplished or lack thereof. The only good thing that Angela had going good in her life was Ashley. She remembered when Ashley was a little girl watching and trying to mimic her every move. It made Angela proud that Ashley had turned into one of the world's best agents and used the skills that she had instilled in her for good instead of evil. Angela may have been locked up but that didn't stop her from training the best she could twice a day. She made sure she kept her body in the best shape, by running five miles a day, and doing calisthenics pushing her body to the limit. Angela was just about to head to the shower when a C.O. Aggressively banged on her cell door.

"Angela you have a visitor!" The male C.O. barked.

"A visitor?" Angela echoed. In her entire eight years of being incarcerated, she'd yet to have a visitor. The only person that would be coming to visit Angela was Ashley, but due to her job, she wasn't allowed to visit. Ashley even had to secretly write Angela under a false name. "You sure?"

"Yes I'm sure now put a shirt on and let's go!"

Angela quickly threw her facility issued shirt on and followed the C.O. down to the visiting room. Her antennas went up when she noticed they had walked pass the visiting room. She was about to ask a question, but decided to just remain silence and see how this played out. The C.O. Lead Angela into a small room. The first person she noticed was the warden followed by a tall white man in an expensive suit, and standing next to him was

34

a woman dressed in a nice pants suit and a banging pair of heels. Upon further review, Angela noticed that the woman in the pants suit looked awfully familiar. "Ashley?" She said in a light whisper.

"Hey Angela," Ashley smiled as the two ran and gave each other the biggest bear hug ever.

"I thought I would never see you again," Angela took a step back to look at Ashley as a few tears ran down her face. "Look at you all grown now."

"I hate to rain on you two's parade but we need to get down to business," Captain Spiller said in a stern tone.

Angela wiped her eyes helped herself to a seat at the table. Whatever was going on she knew it had to be bad if Ashley was here.

"Well it's like this," Ashley began. "One of the biggest terrorist has his crosshairs on me because I killed his son, and I'm this close to taking him down," Ashley said holding her fingers inches apart from each other. "The only problem is Abdul is in so many people's pockets I don't know who to trust."

"Okay so what does this have to do with me?" Angela asked.

"I can trust you so I was thinking..."

"No!" Angela cut her off. "If this is what ya'll came up here for ya'll wasted a trip."

"Listen Angela I don't have time to play with you!" Captain Spiller barked. "I don't like you! Nor do I need you, but for some strange reason Ashley here thinks you can help her take Abdul down, the choice is yours either you in or you out?"

"Count me out," Angela pushed away from the table and headed for the door.

"Angela wait!" Ashley called out. "If you walk out that door I'm as good as dead, I really need your help."

"You're the best agent in the world how could you possibly need my help?" Angela turned to walk out the door.

"Mr. Death is on his way to the states right now!" Ashley said. The mention of Mr. Death's name caused Angela to stop dead in her tracks. "Mr. Death and Abdul are working on something really big and I really need your help Angela...please."

"Ashley why would you come here and get me involved in something like this?" Angela asked. "I haven't held a gun in over eight years, haven't even got into as much as a fist fight going on ten years, I'm not sure if I'll be of any help to you."

"C'mon," Ashley smirked. "It's like riding a bike, something you just don't forget how to do."

"If I say yes what happens to my charges?" Angela asked. "Once this mission is over will I be a free woman again?"

"Depends," Captain Spiller said. "If you succeed on this mission when it's over you'll have two choices one you can report back to jail immediately or two," he paused. "You can work for our agency full time and be partners with Agent Brown."

Angela thought about it for a second. She was damned if she did and damned if she didn't. A part of her was a little nervous especially since it had been almost a decade since the last time she had any type of physical activity. The last thing she wanted to do was go out there and get Ashley killed. "I don't know," she said doubtfully. "What if I don't have it no more?"

"You were the best!" Ashley reminded her. "Angela I know you don't really want any parts of this, but if you don't help me I'm as good as dead."

"I'm in," Angela said. Immediately Ashley ran over and hugged her tightly.

"Thank you, thank you, and thank you!" Ashley had never been this happy in her life. Not only would she be taking down one of the biggest terrorist to ever walk the earth, but also on top of that she had managed to get her mentor her freedom for the time being.

"I need two weeks of training to get back into the swing of things," Angela said.

"No can do!" Captain Spiller's voice boomed. "The mission goes down tomorrow!"

# CHAPTER |4 MR. DEATH

Mr. Death entered the vacant apartment that rested directly across the street from the building in which the diamonds were being held in. Lieutenant Banks had told Abdul exactly where to find the diamonds, now it was Mr. Death's job to go and retrieve them. Mr. Death was a clean-cut Japanese man in his early thirties he was dressed in an all-black ninja suit. He sat his duffle bag down and quickly removed the sniper rifle and assemble it in fifteen seconds flat. Mr. Death set his rifle up on the window seal and looked through the scope. The first target was an overweight man in the next building who sat on the couch eating from a container of Chinese food. The second target was an elderly black man who seemed to be in what looked like a heated conversation on his cell phone. The third and final target was focused on something on his laptop. Mr. Death focused for no longer than ten seconds before he squeezed down on the trigger three times in rapid succession. The shots from the rifle sounded like three keys being pressed on a type writer. Across the street in the next building, three agents laid dead in a puddle of their own blood. Mr. Death quickly left the apartment and headed over to the building across the street. Lieutenant Banks had told him that there would be five agents in total guarding the diamonds which meant that there were two more agents somewhere within the vicinity. Mr. Death entered the apartment building with a 9mm with a silencer attached to the barrel in his hand. The gun held sixteen shots, but he wouldn't need anymore more than two shots to finish this job. Mr. Death jogged up the stairs with the quietness of a cat until he reached the fourth floor. Mr. Death sprung from the staircase out into the hallway. Two agents stood guarding a door at the end of the hall. Mr. Death quickly put the two agents down, shot the lock off the front door, and entered the apartment. He swiftly moved to the back room to the safe right where Lieutenant Banks told him it would be. Mr. Death punched in the combination retrieved the diamonds and just like that, he was gone. The warm up was done now it was time for him to get his next mission started.

# CHAPTER

**5** READY OR NOT

A ngela sat on the plane staring blankly out the window. Her mind was telling her that she was making a terrible decision, but her heart was telling her otherwise. Angela loved Ashley like a daughter and planned on doing her best to keep her alive. During the flight, Captain Spiller had given her a file on the man they called Mr. Death and told her everything he knew about the assassin. "So what's the plan?"

"We just got word that Mr. Death called an escort service requesting a blonde for the night," Captain Spiller began. "We're going to have Ashley dress up like an escort and eliminate the target."

"Are you insane?" Angela asked. "I'm not going to sit back and let you send her in on suicide mission."

"You have a better plan?" Captain Spiller spat. "I didn't think so," he said not giving Angela a chance to answer. "This is the only opportunity we have to eliminate this bastard."

"You okay with this?" Angela asked looking over at Ashley.

"I think I can take this guy," Ashley said confidently. She sat across from Angela loading her Five-seven pistol. She was confident in her skills and was ready to put them up to the test.

"I just think it's really risky that's all."

"Has prison turned you soft?" Captain Spiller said looking Angela up and down. "I thought you were supposed to be the best."

"I was the best," Angela countered.

"Then start acting like it, damn it!" Captain Spiller barked.

"Okay that's enough!" Ashley jumped in. "We all on the same team!"

Angela rolled her eyes and focused back on looking out the window. From that moment forth Angela decided to just keep her mouth shut, she realized she didn't have any say so in the matter so voicing her opinion was pointless. As Angela sat staring out the window, she felt Ashley sit next to her.

"We can take this guy I know we can," Ashley said as she squeezed into a tight fitting red strapless dress. The plane would be landing in an hour, from the airport she would have to run across town to meet Mr. Death at his hotel room and get the mission started.

"Ashley I just don't want you to get hurt that's all," Angela said. "I have all the confidence in the world in you, but I'm still a bit nervous. If something happens to you I'll never be able to forgive myself," she explained.

"I'll be fine," Ashley smiled as a team of makeup artist began working on Ashley's face.

An hour later, the plane landed and Ashley stepped off the plane looking like an entirely different person. The red dress, blonde wig, and all the makeup gave her a stunning look. She turned to Angela. "How do I look?"

"Like a high priced prostitute," Angela said seriously.

Ashley handed her an ear wig. "Here put that on and let me know if you can hear me, testing one, and two."

"Can hear you loud and clear," Angela replied.

"Okay it's show time," Ashley said with a nervous smile.

"Wish me luck."

"Good luck, and please know that I'll only be a couple of feet away," Angela looked Ashley in the eyes letting her know that no matter what she had her back.

"This'll be a piece of cake," Ashley smiled as she disappeared in the back seat of the awaiting limousine.

"I hope so," Angela said as she watched the limousine pull off. She then quickly hopped in the back of the awaiting van along with Captain Spiller, and Troy.

# CHAPTER

**6** NO TURNING BACK

All types of thoughts ran through Ashley's mind as she sat in the back seat of the limousine. Mr. Death was supposed to be the real deal and one of the world's best assassins; today Ashley would find out just how good she was. A small .22 caliber pistol that was strapped to her inner thigh and a four inch blade that rested in Ashley's purse were the only weapons that she had. She stepped out of the limousine and entered the five star hotel, the butterflies in her stomach were doing summersaults.

"Relax," Ashley could hear Angela's voice through the ear piece. "Just another day at the office."

"I'm nervous and my palms are sweating," Ashley said as she

boarded the empty elevator and pressed the 10th floor.

"Just relax and know that we are right outside the hotel if you need us," Angela reminded her.

"Thanks," Ashley replied as she stepped off the elevator and proceeded down the hall towards Mr. Death's room. She reached the room and knocked lightly on the door. Seconds later a Japanese man answered the door dressed in an expensive looking navy blue suit, and covering his hands were a pair of black leather gloves.

"Mr. Wang?" Ashley asked.

"Yes I am Mr. Wang," he smiled while giving Ashley the once over from head to toe.

"May I come inside?" Ashley asked with a seductive smile.

"I would like for you to join me for dinner first," Mr. Death said.

"That's fine but you do know that I charge by the hour."

"Money will not be an issue," Mr. Death smiled as he led Ashley down the hall and back onto the elevated.

"You're doing real well, just stay focused, and relax," Angela

47

voice buzzed into Ashley's ear piece.

Ashley slid into the passenger seat of the B.M.W and made sure she crossed her leg to show off her heavily oiled calf muscle and part of her thighs. On the ride to the restaurant, Ashley made small talk with the man that she was hired to kill before the night was out.

Mr. Death and Ashley stepped foot in the fancy restaurant and were quickly escorted to a table over in the cut.

"Will you be having the usual sir?" The waitress asked in a polite tone.

"Yes ma'am," Mr. Death replied with a head nod. He then turned his attention to Ashley. "So tell me a little about yourself."

"Well I'm 23 years old; I like to have fun, eat good food, and enjoy myself. Besides that I live a pretty much boring life," Ashley lied. She was supposed to kill Mr. Death in his hotel room but instead here she was having dinner with him making small talk.

"You seem like a nice girl why you are out here selling your body?" Mr. Death asked as the waitress returned and sat a bottle of red wine down on the table.

Ashley shrugged. "I need the money."

"Why not get a job?"

"I have no skills," Ashley replied.

Mr. Death went to reach for the bottle of wine, but accidentally knocked his glass off the table. With the reflexes of a cat, Ashley caught the glass before it hit the floor. Her reflexes caused Mr. Death to look at her with a suspicious eye.

"Here, have some wine," Mr. Death poured Ashley a glass and slid it in her direction.

"No thank you," Ashley declined. She needed to have a clear mind if she planned to pull of the mission at hand.

"No I insist," Mr. Death pushed the glass towards her.

Ashley grabbed the glass and looked in it making sure she didn't see nothing floating around or fizzling inside the glass. "Are you going to have a drink with me?"

"I don't drink," Mr. Death, answered quickly.

"Do not drink that wine it's probably spiked with something!" Angela's voice chirped through Ashley's ear piece.

Ashley didn't want to drink the wine but she knew if she didn't it would surely cause Mr. Death to become suspicious. Going against better judgment Ashley sipped the wine. As the night went on, Ashley continued to sip from her glass while the two enjoyed their dinner. Ashley went to say something when all of a sudden the effects from the wine started to kick in. "Whew!" She huffed.

"Are you alright?" Mr. Death asked faking concern.

"This wine is very strong," Ashley hinted. As the place slowly began to spin.

"It's the best wine that money can buy," Mr. Death said with a smirk. He wasn't big on trust and always thought that someone was out to kill him, so whenever Mr. Death came this restaurant he had the waitress spike the wine with a substance that made whoever drank it incoherent.

"Excuse me for a second," Ashley said as she got up and staggered towards the ladies room. "Shit he slipped something in my drink," Ashley said as soon as she stepped foot in the restroom.

"Can you see?" Angela's voice chirped through Ashley's ear piece.

"My vision is a little blurry, but I'm okay," Ashley lied.

"We're coming in to get you," Angela said in a worried tone.

"No I'm fine I can handle it," Ashley told her. She wanted to splash some water on her face but didn't want to ruin her make up in the process. "I'm going to wrap it up here and head back to his room so I can seal this deal."

Ashley slowly walked back over to the talk and sat down.

"Is everything alright?" Mr. Death asked with a normal expression on his face. There was something fishy about the woman that sat across from him he just couldn't figure out what, but he was sure to get down to the bottom of it.

"Yes I'm fine," Ashley put on a fake smile. "I'm ready to get out of here and get my hands on you," she licked her lips seductively.

Mr. Death smiled, stood to his feet, then lead Ashley out of the restaurant. Ashley sunk down in the passenger seat of the B.M.W and immediately felt nauseous. She felt that at any second she was going to throw up, the motion from the car was not helping her one bit. Ashley's vision wasn't getting any better either which meant that she would have to make her move as soon as she entered the room. She knew she was at a disadvantage now, but felt as if this was her one and only chance to throw a monkey wrench in Abdul's big plan so she decided to go along with it.

* * *

"I think we should pull her from the mission," Angela suggested. She knew Ashley was a soldier and would rather die in the field rather than be removed from a mission, but now she wasn't in her right state of mind and that's what concerned Angela.

"She said she's fine," Captain Spiller said. His main concern was accomplishing the mission at hand.

"She's been drugged for God's sake!" Angela shouted.

"I said she's fine!" Captain Spiller barked. "Now that's the end of it!"

# CHAPTER

## 7 WALKING BLIND

Ashley entered the hotel room and immediately kicked off her heels. She wanted to be comfortable and prepared for what she knew was soon to come.

"Let's get down to it," Mr. Death said as he unzipped his zipper, pulled his manhood through the hole, and began stroking it right in front of Ashley.

Ashley swallowed hard when she looked down at Mr. Death's nice sized penis. Her mouth instantly began to water along with the sweet spot that was between her thighs. In her line of work, she rarely had time for a relationship, so the site of a nice sized package had Ashley thinking about sampling the product. "I just need a second to freshen up," Ashely said, then disappeared inside the bathroom. Once inside the bathroom, Ashley removed her .22, cocked a round into the chamber, took a deep breath, and then stepped back out the bathroom with a firm one handed grip on her weapon. Ashley tip-toed back out to where she had left Mr. Death standing and pause when she realized he was no longer standing there. The suite they were in was so big, that meant he could have been anywhere. Ashley slowly and cautiously inched her way through the suite until she noticed movement coming from her right. Out of nowhere, a foot kicked Ashley's gun out of her hand. Before she got a chance to react, Mr. Death landed a stiff jab to the center of her face causing her head to violently snap back, he then grabbed her arm and roughly hip-tossed her. Ashley's body came crashing down onto the glass coffee table sending glass shattering everywhere. Once Ashley's back hit the floor, her legs popped up and grabbed Mr. Death's head in a scissor lock. Ashley tried to strangle Mr. Death with her muscular thighs.

Mr. Death effortlessly grabbed Ashley's legs and spun around violently, tossing her upper body into the wall causing her to release her grip. Ashley quickly hopped to her feet and took her fighting stance.

Mr. Death took one look at Ashley's fighting stance and smirked. Ashley went to throw a punch, but a kick to the side of her face staggered her. The kick happened so fast that she never saw it coming. Mr. Death slowly walked towards Ashley with his hands down. She threw a series of blows, but none came near to landing, Mr. Death blocked all the blows and landed a stiff closed back hand to Ashley's face. Ashley attempted to deliver a side kick, but Mr. Death easily side stepped the kick and swept her other leg from up under her. Mr. Death patiently allowed Ashley a chance to get up. Ashley made it back to her feet grabbed her purse from off the couch and pulled out her knife.

Blood dripped from Ashley's nose as she slowly inched her way towards Mr. Death. She realized that her skills were no match for the assassin, especially with her not functioning at a hundred percent. Ashley fainted with the knife repeatedly before finally making a move. She tried to jab the knife in Mr. Death's chest, but he caught her wrist before the blade even got close to touching his skin, with his free hand he landed an open-palm blow to Ashley's forehead, grabbed Ashley's knife hand, and snapped the bone at the elbow all in one quick motion.

"Aaaaaarghhhh!" Ashley yelled in severe pain. Mr. Death followed up with a quick six punch combo that landed in Ashley's chest and face. His hands moved as fast as lightening, as if he was a star actor in a kung fu movie. Ashley hit the floor hard, rolled over, grabbed her gun from up off the floor and came up firing.

POW! POW! POW! POW!

Mr. Death ran through the hotel room dodging bullets and quickly dived over the couch.

* * *

Angela sat in the back of the van listening with a scared and worried look on her face as the violent fight continued to take place in the hotel room. Just from the sound of the battle, Angela could tell that Ashley was on the losing end of the fight. Angela jumped in her seat when she heard Ashley roar with a pain-filled scream.

"I'm going in!" Angela said as she grabbed Troy's 9mm from

off his waist, hopped out the back of the van, and jogged into the five star hotel. She could no longer sit back and let this continue. Captain Spiller looked over at Troy. "Go after and make sure she's alright." he ordered.

# CHAPTER

**8** WHAT HAVE I GOTTEN
MYSELF INTO

Ashley inched her way through the hotel room when she heard the bathroom door slam. She was determined to kill Mr. Death especially after the bad ass beaten he had just gave her. Ashley looked down at her arm and stringed when she saw her bone poking through her stink, she had never experienced this type of pain in her life. Ashley turned the corner and eyed the closed bathroom door.

"Stay where you are. I'm on my way up now! Ashley heard Angela's voice through her ear piece.

"I have him trapped in the bathroom I'm going in!"

"No wait for me!" Angela pressed.

Ashley ignored her mentor and continued towards the bathroom. On the silent count of three, Ashley came forward and kicked the bathroom door open.

In a flash, Mr. Death sprang from the bathroom, grabbed the wrist of Ashley's gun hand, jammed a sharp five in blade in the pit of her stomach, and twisted the handle. Ashley squeezed down on the trigger repeatedly sending shots through the wall and ceiling until her gun was empty.

Mr. Death coolly exited the hotel room leaving Ashley in the room to die. Not even breaking a sweat Mr. Death smoothly disappeared in the staircase.

* * *

Angela stepped off the elevator with her gun drawn and held it in a steady two handed grip. She knew the man that they called Mr. Death was supposed to be a beast so she made sure she took caution. Angela entered the room and the first thing she saw was Ashley laying in the middle of the floor in a pool of her own blood. She quickly ran over and kneeled down by Ashley's side.

"Hang in there."

"I'm fine," Ashley, flashed a bloody smile. "Go catch him he took the stairs," she whispered.

"I'm not leaving you," Angela told her.

"I'm fine," Ashley repeated. "Go catch that son of a bitch and make him pay for what he did to me."

Angela looked down into Ashley eyes and could see the passion behind them. Right on, queue Troy entered the hotel room. "Get her some help I'm going after him!" Angela said as she ran straight for the staircase.

"Angela!" Captain Spiller's voice boomed through her ear piece.

"Yeah?"

"I have an eye on Mr. Death. I'm going to follow him."

Angela emerged from the staircase and sprinted through the lobby. "I'm outside, where is he?"

"He just hopped in a black B.M.W heading north!" Captain Spiller replied.

"Shit!" Angela cursed as she looked around for a vehicle she could take. Coming down the street was a guy riding a motorcycle. Angela ran out into the street and aimed the gun at the rider. "I need your bike!"

The rider quickly did as he was told and handed over his bike and helmet. Angela threw the helmet on, hopped on the bike, and dramatically spun her tires as she peeled off.

"Where is he?" Angela asked as the motorcycle, roared, and vibrated between her legs, as it picked up speed.

"Make a left!" Captain Spiller's voice chirped in Angela's ear piece. Angela quickly made a left and spotted the black B.M.W a few blocks away. Angela weaved from lane to lane as images of Ashley's bruised and bloodied face kept popping up in her head. Angela rolled on the driver side of the B.M.W and shot out the window. Immediately, the B.M.W swerved over two lanes and gunned the engine.

Mr. Death made a sharp left turn down a one way street. He didn't know who the gunman on the motorcycle was but it really made no difference to him. He kept a calm look on his face as he maneuvered the B.M.W with one hand while his other hand rested on his P89 with the silencer attached to the barrel. Mr.

Death kept his eyes in the rear view mirror making sure he kept the gunman at a reasonable distance. Mr. Death wasn't expecting this ambush. He had come to the states to do a job, and the interference was becoming somewhat of an annoyance. Whoever the gunman on the motorcycle was, was soon about to be eliminated.

Mr. Death quickly stomped down on the brakes, cut the wheel hard to the left. The B.M.W fishtailed spinning around. Mr. Death then quickly threw the gear in reverse and stepped down hard on the gas pedal. He stuck his arm out the window and fired off four shots in rapid succession, while the B.M.W flew backwards in reverse.

"Shit!" Angela cursed as she leaned to the right and bunny hopped up on the curb to avoid the bullets that Mr. Death sent her way. The motorcycle zoomed down the side walk as Angela stay hunched down low using the parked cars that was lined up alongside the street as her shield.

Once the gunman on bike was out of Mr. Death's view, he quickly cut the wheel to the right, stomped down on the brakes, tossed the gear back in drive, and continued on down the street at a high speed. Mr. Death made sharp turn after sharp turn in hopes of shaking the gunman on the bike but it was no use, every time he looked through the rear view mirror, the gunman on the bike was right there.

Angela aimed her 9mm at the back tire of the B.M.W and pulled the trigger. Seconds later she watched the B.M.W wildly spin out of control, bounced off a light pole, and parked car.

The motorcycle came to a skidding stop as Angela quickly hopped off the bike and began making her way towards the B.M.W with a two handed grip on her weapon. Angela made it a few feet away from the B.M.W, when suddenly it began to pour down raining. Angela snatched the driver's door open with her finger wrapped around the trigger of her weapon ready to fire, but paused when she saw that the vehicle was empty.

"What the fuck?" Angela asked with a confused look on her face. She stood there for a second, trying to figure out where Mr. Death could have gone when she spotted movement out the corner of her eye. To her left, she saw a figure quickly dip inside a rundown looking bar. Angela quickly jogged over towards the entrance of the bar and snatched the door open. She stepped foot in the bar and immediately all eyes were on her. The few patrons that occupied the bar all looked as if they had seen a ghost.

"Which way did he go?" Angela asked. The bartender quickly nodded towards the back exit. Angela headed towards the back exit and kicked the door open. Through the back door was a dark alley. Angela stepped out the door when a foot came out of nowhere and kicked her gun out of her hands. Another kick was aimed for Angela's face, but she quickly blocked the kick, held on to Mr. Death's leg, and rushed him backwards. Immediately, the two went tumbling violently down the stairs and down into the alley. Angela landed on top and quickly began to rain punches down on Mr. Death's face. One punch landed before he flipped Angela up off of him. Mr. Death made it to his feet, whipped his gun out of its holster with a snap, and fired off two shots in Angela's direction.

Pst! Pst!

Angela dove behind a dumpster as the bullets pinged loudly off the huge metal trash bin. Without thinking twice, Angela pulled out her back up .380. She couldn't see Mr. Death but she could somewhat pin point his location by the sound of his shoes

64

making contact with the concrete. Angela listened carefully then sprung from behind the dumpster and fired off a shot. With the reflexes of a snake, Mr. Death front flip rolled and came up firing. Angela quickly got back behind the dumpster just as the bullets pinged loudly and ricocheted off of it.

Mr. Death touched his cheek and his hand came away bloody.

The shot that Angela fired had grazed his cheek, another inch closer and his brains would have been all over the alley. Immediately, Mr. Death's competitive spirit kicked and he wanted to show the lady assassin that he was indeed the better assassin. Just as Mr. Death went to move in for the kill, a black van came flying down the alley full speed. Mr. Death had no other choice then to flee the scene. He took off down the alley and quickly bent the corner.

The black van came to a screeching stop directly in front of

Angela. The door to the van slid open and Captain Spiller stuck his head out the door. "Get in!"

Angela quickly hopped in the back of the van as it pulled off dramatically. "Don't lose him."

"I got him," the driver said with confidence.

"Where's Ashley?" Angela asked.

"She's being taking to the hospital as we speak," Captain Spiller told her and left it at that.

# CHAPTER

**9** I REFUSE TO QUIT

M r. Death power walked down the street looking for an escape route. He knew he didn't have much time from how loud the sound of the sirens were becoming. As he crossed the street, the same black van came spilling wildly out into the street. Mr. Death pulled his P89 from his shoulder holster and fired three shots into the windshield seconds later; he watched the van spun out of control, hop the curb, and crash head first into a building.

Mr. Death smiled when he saw the van crash into the building. That smile was quickly erased from his face when he heard a voice yell, "Freeze!" From behind him.

"Drop your weapon...now!" The officer yelled with his gun train at Mr. Death's head while his partner backed him up.

Mr. Death slowly place his gun down on the concrete and put his hands behind his back. The officer quickly cuffed him and roughly forced him to sit on the concrete Indian-style. Mr. Death snapped his thumb out of place and began to slip his hand out of the cuffs while the two officers searched him and waited for back up to arrive.

"Put this jackass in the back of the car until back up gets here," the lead officer ordered. His partner roughly grabbed Mr. Death and pulled him up to his feet. Once on his feet, Mr. Death slipped his hand free from the cuffs and chopped the officer in the throat, when the officer reached to grab his throat with both hands; Mr. Death grabbed the officer's 9mm from his holster and blew his brains out in the middle of the street. Before his body could even hit the ground Mr. Death turned the gun from that officer over to the lead officer all in one quick motion, seconds later his brain popped out the back of his skull like a jack in the box. He gunned the two cops down so easily one would have

68

thought he was playing a video game.

Mr. Death jumped in the front seat of the squad car and pulled away from the scene just as several other cops cars pulled up to the scene.

\* \* \*

Angela and Captain Spiller crawled from the van and refused medical attention. At that moment, Captain Spiller knew that they had just messed up big time. The plan was to eliminate Mr. Death tonight so he wouldn't be able to go through with his plan but they had failed. Now all they could do was wait until the assassin decided to strike again and hope pray that they'd be able to stop him.

"Now what?" Angela asked with blood trickling from her forehead. She had banged her head hard during the crash.

"The only thing we can do now is wait," Captain Spiller said with a defeated look on his face.

# CHAPTER

**10** SURPRISE, SURPRISE

Lieutenant Banks was awaken from his sleep with a barrel pressed to his head. His eyes snapped open and all that could be seen in them was fear. "Mr... Mr... Mr. Death what are you doing here?" he stuttered.

"The two women who are they and why wasn't I notified about them?" Mr. Death asked.

"The first girl is Ashley and she one of our best agents," Lieutenant Banks mumbled.

"And the other chick?"

"Some chick called the Teflon Queen."

"As in thee Teflon queen?" Mr. Death asked. He had heard

several stories about the so called Teflon queen; the main story was how she had more lives than a cat. Last, he had heard she was rotting in some prison somewhere unknown. "When she start working for your agency?"

"She doesn't," Lieutenant Banks spat. "That bitch Ashley went over my head and somehow got her involved."

"You are being paid a lot of money to make things easier for me, either you do your job or the next time I see you I'll do mines," Mr. Death threatened him.

"I promise something like this won't happen again," Lieutenant Banks assured him. "What's next?"

"Wouldn't you love to know," Mr. Death smiled as he placed his gun back in its holster and made his exit. He didn't trust Lieutenant Banks one bit and planned on killing him as soon as his work in the states were done, just because.

# CHAPTER

**11** WHAT'S THE PLAN?

Captain Spiller and Angela made their way back to Mr. Death's hotel to look around and hopefully find some clues. Several other officers walked around the room with latex gloves covering their hands. The officers flipped the mattress, looked through draws, and even closets. The only thing they found so far were plenty of weapons and ammunition. Angela walked over towards the safe in the room. "Hey get somebody in here that can open this," they had searched every inch of the room the only place they hadn't looked was in the safe. Minutes later, a manager entered the room and handed Captain Spiller a piece a paper that held the combination to the safe on it.

Captain Spiller slowly pressed the numbers into the key pad and instantly, the safe's door snapped open. Inside the safe was a folder with a few papers inside. Captain Spiller sat down and began going through the documents. "Jesus Christ," he whispered, then handed the documents over to Angela so she could look over them.

Angela glanced at the documents and shook her head in disgust. "He's going to try to kill the president," she announced. In her hands were blue prints to every entrance and exit to the White House, along with several photos of the president and the First Lady. "I've got to stop him,"

"How do you plan on doing that?" Captain Spiller asked.

"I need to be around the president twenty-four hours a day until Mr. Death is either killed or captured," Angela said.

"The Secret Service are more than capable of protecting the president," Captain Spiller countered. He knew that it wasn't likely that the president would agree to allow Angela to shadow him around twenty four hours a day, but it was worth a try.

"I need you to get us a meeting with the president before it's too late," Angela said in a serious tone. She could tell by her first encounter with Mr. Death that he wasn't the type of guy to take lightly; he was highly skilled and much disciplined.

"I'll do my best," Captain Spiller said as he noticed Angela heading for the door. "And where do you think you're going?"

"To go check up on Ashley," Angela said, then disappeared out the door.

# CHAPTER

## 12 I'M SORRY

Ashley laid up in the hospital bed with a defeated look on her face. Her confidence was shot and she felt as if she had let her team down. Most importantly, she had failed in front of her mentor. By her bedside sat Troy. He had been by Ashley's side all the way through and unlike everyone else, he still believed in her.

"What you over there thinking about?" Troy asked, snapping Ashley out of her thoughts.

"About how I let everyone down," Ashley admitted.

"Listen we all know this is a rough and dangerous business," Troy said. "And trust me you'll get another shot at this guy."

"But what if I fail again?"

"You won't fail again," Angela said, stepping into the room. Ashley noticed the fresh scars on Angela's face and knew that she had indeed caught up with Mr. Death.

"Did you get him?" Ashley asked.

"No he got away," Angela said. "What are your damages looking like?"

"Broken arm and a few minor bruises, nothing serious," Ashley flashed a smile. "I kind of feel like I let you down."

"That's nonsense he drugged you and you weren't in your right frame of mind," Angela reminded her. She knew that Ashley had the skills along with the brains to take anyone down and complete any mission. "Rest up because I'm going to need your help."

"What's up?"

"We found documents informing us that Mr. Death is going to try and take out the president," Angela told her.

"Do you know when?"

"No we have no idea," Angela said honestly.

"I'm looking forward to running into Mr. Death again," Ashley said. The way he had easily beat her up and avoided capture was really taking a toll on her mentally.

"You just focus on getting well and I promise I'll save some action for you," Angela said with a wink.

"You promise?"

"I promise," Angela said as she turned and left.

On the cab ride to her hotel room, Angela had plenty of time to think. She didn't even have time to enjoy her freedom and the fact that she didn't have to be told when to eat or when to sleep. Instead, her mind was on Mr. Death, and the way in which she was going to stop whatever his plans. The documents that they obtained from Mr. Death's hotel room said that the president was the next target. Mr. Death had come to the states to do some serious damage. When Angela had first signed on to help stop Mr. Death, it was business, but not anymore. Mr. Death not only assaulted and hospitalized Ashley but now he was trying to kill the president. This was no longer business for Angela it was now personal. First thing in the morning, Angela and Captain Spiller were headed to Washington DC to take a trip to the White House.

Angela stepped foot in her hotel room and quickly swept the room to make sure she was alone. She then checked the phone, smoke detector, and anything else that might pose as a bug or listening device. Once she was sure that she had her privacy, Angela quickly stripped down and hopped in the shower. It had been years since she had the pleasure to shower alone and without shower slippers on her feet. Angela let the water run down her face and head. After her shower, Angela walked around her room nude. She wasn't sure when the next time she would have the opportunity to do something as small as this so she decided to take full advantage of the situation. Angela placed her 9mm on the night stand, laid sloppily across the bed and watched TV until her eyes became too heavy to keep open.

# CHAPTER

**13** THE WHITE HOUSE

The next morning Angela was awoken by a loud heavy knock on her door. Out of reflex, Angela jumped up, grabbed her 9mm off the night stand, and inched her way towards the door. Her bare breast bouncing with each step she took. Angela peeped through the peep hole and saw Captain Spiller standing on the other side of the door. "Hold on let me throw something on real quick," she yelled as she quickly went and threw her same clothes on from last night.

Angela opened the door and stepped to the side so Captain Spiller could enter. She noticed that in his hand he carried a duffle bag.

"You ready to go meet the president?" Captain Spiller asked with a worried look on his face. His appearance told Angela that he hadn't slept all night. In his hand was a cup from Starbucks.

"Ready as I'm ever going to be," Angela replied. Never in a million years would she have thought that she would ever be meeting the president of the United States, let alone trying to save his life.

"Here I brought you a present," Captain Spiller handed her the duffle bag. Angela took the duffle bag, sat it down on the bed, and then looked inside. Inside the duffle bag was a bullet proof vest, two Five-seven hand guns, a hunting knife, and a backup .25.

"Thank you so much," Angela smiled as she rushed off to the bathroom to strap on her bullet proof vest. She emerged from the bathroom feeling like a new woman. "Ok now let's do this,"

\* \* \*

Captain Spiller and Angela boarded the helicopter and headed to the nation's capital. During the ride, Angela enjoyed the view of all the cities they passed. During the ride, Captain Spiller repeated over and over that when they arrived at the White House that he was to do all the talking. When the helicopter landed, Captain Spiller and Angela were immediately met by four Secret Service agents.

"Right this way," The Secret Service agents said, leading the couple inside the White House. Angela looked on in awe as she got a brief tour of the historic home of all the past Presidents. As she walked past looking at all the history, she knew right then and there that she couldn't allow the president to be killed.

The Secret Service agents lead Captain Spiller and Angela into the president's office. The president sat behind his desk on the phone with three Secret Service agents standing close by.

When the president was done with his phone call, he stood up, flashed a bright smile, and walked from around his desk. "Hi you it's nice to meet you," he said as he shook both Captain Spiller and Angela's hand. "Now how can I help you two," he asked as he walked back around his desk and took a seat.

Captain Spiller cleared his throat. "Sir we have reason to believe that an attack is being planned," he began. "I and my team have come across some information that you may find helpful," he handed the folder to the head Secret Service agent a man that went by the name Steve. "It seems as if Abdul has hired an elite assassin to assassinate you Mr. President."

Steve looked at the documents closely then handed them over to the president. The president took a minute to read over the documents. "Thank you for this information, I appreciate your time Captain Spiller but I believe me and my men can take it from here."

"You're welcome Mr. President," Captain Spiller said with a head nod then turned to leave. That was until Angela spoke up.

"Um excuse me Mr. President Sir but I was wondering maybe if you would allow me to somehow help out with your security," Angela spoke up.

"And you are?"

"Angela but most people know me as the Teflon Queen Sir."

"The Teflon Queen?" The president repeated as he began thinking about where he had heard the name. "The assassin that was wanted for a number of years?"

"Yes sir that would be me," Angela said proudly.

"How did you get out of jail?"

"Sir I no longer work for the other side. I'm one of the good guys now and whether you know it or not you need my help."

"The president is in good hands," Steve said, speaking for the first time. He was the lead agent and head of the president's security and didn't like how Angela had come in acting as if he would allow the president to lose his life.

"No disrespect to you," Angela said looking over at Steve.

"But the man that's out to kill the president is in a class of his own. He's highly skilled and loves to kill."

"And so am I!" Steve shot back.

"Listen, Mr. President," Angela said turning her focus back on him. "Just the fact that I'm even here means that you're in big trouble," she told him. "I understand that Steve is in charge and the head of your security, all I'm asking is that you bring me aboard for no longer than a month. It probably won't even take a month because the assassin is already here and trust and believe he's here for a reason."

"I have a problem putting my life in the hands of an ex

criminal," the president said honestly. "And if you haven't noticed my security is tight. The Secret Service is trained to protect and to kill for me, so I do appreciate your offer of protection, but I'm going to have to pass."

"Thank you for your time Mr. President," Captain Spiller said as he grabbed Angela by the wrist and lead her out the same way they had come in. Once back outside Captain Spiller turned his attention to Angela, "I thought I told you to keep your mouth shut and let me do all the talking?" He scolded. "You think the president wants an ex criminal protecting him? No! If you would have just kept your mouth shut I could of still gotten you in!"

"The president needed to know how much danger he was in," Angela said. She couldn't just sit back and let the president walk blindly into a pool of violence that was sure to come.

"The whole purpose of us coming down here was to help protect the president," Captain Spiller reminded her.

"And that's just what I'm going to do," Angela stated firmly. She refused to take 'no' for an answer and refused to just sit back and allow the president to get assassinated.

84

"What's going on in that head of yours?" Captain Spiller asked. He could see the wheels in Angela's head turning.

"It looks like I'm just going to have to keep a close eye on the president myself," Angela stated plainly.

"Do what you have to do," Captain Spiller said. They had come too far to go back empty handed now. For some strange reason Captain Spiller had a gut feeling that Mr. Death would definitely be coming for the president sooner than later.

# CHAPTER

**14** PROTECTION

Mr. Death walked smoothly down the subway platform. He hated New York City because of how crowded it was. The people were rude and they all had bad nasty attitudes and seemed to be in a rush to go nowhere. However, as bad he hated New York he had to be there today. Today was the day that the president was going to die. The president was scheduled to show up and give a speech at a charity event for handicapped children.

Mr. Death waited for the train to pass, then smoothly hopped down on the track, and took off in a light jog down the tunnel. He jogged until he reached a door. He quickly shot the lock off and entered what looked to be a sewer. Mr. Death pulled out a pen flashlight and shined the light down on a map. The map was going to lead him directly underneath the building where the charity event would take place. A smirk crawled on his lips as he followed the directions on the map carefully.

* * *

Angela stepped foot inside the building that the charity event was being held and the first thing she noticed was that the place was locked down with security which was a good sign. The second thing that she noticed was that the building only had two exit points so if something was to go down she was looking for the quickest exit route possible. Disguised in her vintage blonde wig and sun glasses Angela stood over in the corner out of site. The security was so good that she wasn't allowed to enter with her weapon. Her plan was to keep a close eye on the president and hope and pray that nothing bad happened and nobody got hurt.

Angela watched as Steve and three other Secret Service agents shadowed the president's every move as he walked around smiling and shaking everyone's hand. The president made his way around the room and stopped when he came across Angela.

"Nice to meet y..." His words got caught in his throat when he realized whose hand he was shaking. "What are you doing here?" He growled in a strong whisper while smiling the entire time.

"I'm just here to watch your back sir," Angela said replied matching his smile.

"I don't need you to watch my back

"Sir you are in great danger," Angela told him. "I'm not in you or your staff's way I'm over here in the cut."

"Stay away from me I don't want you nowhere near me you are a criminal and a murderer," the president walked off and left Angela standing there. He made his way over to the podium cleared his throat and began with his speech. Several members of the media began recording and broadcasting the president's speech live.

Angela sat back and kept a close eye on the president. She also noticed Steve giving her dirty looks while the president gave his speech.

* * *

When Mr. Death reached his destination, he quickly removed the book bag from his back. Removed his jacket and slipped into an all-black ninja suit. He placed the ninja mask over his face and all that could be seen were his eyes. He removed a belt from his book bag and placed it around his waist, but this wasn't an ordinary belt this utility belt held tear gas, extra clips of ammo, a hunting knife, and a 9mm that held sixteen shots with a silencer attached to the barrel. Mr. Death removed a block of C-4 from his book bag and tossed it up to the ceiling the sticky gum like residue stuck to the ceiling like glue. Mr. Death took a few steps back and pressed the button on his device that made the C-4 explode.

* * *

Angela stood in her same spot in the corner listening to the president's long speech that was filled with a lot of concern and a few jokes. Overall, the event was kind of on the boring side of things, but she had to be there for a reason. Angela covered her mouth as she yawned, when out of nowhere she heard a loud boom followed by the floor rumbling. Right then and there Angela knew that Mr. Death had arrived.

# CHAPTER | 15 DEATH IN THE AIR

Several Secret Service agents stood around in the basement of the building the charity event was being held lollygagging and sipping coffee. This was the worst part of their job, the sitting around idly waiting. The agents continued to drink coffee when all of a sudden, a loud explosion erupted, and the floor caved in sending every one of the agents violently crashing down to the lower level of the sewer. Once the explosion was over Mr. Death climbed up into the basement, quickly removed his 9mm, and positioned himself by the steps. He got down on one knee and aimed his gun at the closed door. Ten seconds later the door swung open and he fired off three shots in rapid succession. Instantly three bodies came tumbling down the stairs. With the quickness of a rattle snake Mr. Death flew up the stairs skipping two at a time. When he reached the upper level, he sprung out the door. The first agent screamed, "Gun!" He reached for his waistband but a bullet to the throat dropped him. The next agent was able to get off a shot but a bullet punctured his eye and came out through the back of his head sending blood and brains everywhere. Mr. Death then turned his gun on the president and fired off two shots. Steve quickly tackled the president down to the floor as the two shots exploded in the back area of his vest.

Mr. Death spun and took cover behind a wall as the rest of the Secret Service returned fire. He pulled a can of tear gas from his belt and tossed it out into the open, sending the media and small handicap children and parents into a frenzy. Everyone immediately began coughing and trying to cover their mouth and noses. Mr. Death let the clip fall from the base of his gun and quickly replaced it with another one. Mr. Death spun around the corner and put a bullet in the head of the closest agent. His pin point accuracy was beginning to be a real problem for the Secret

Service. A close by guard tried to sneak up on Mr. Death from behind and hit him in the head with a billy club. Mr. Death caught the man's arm in mid swing, twisted his arm snapping it at the elbow he then placed the barrel of his gun under the man's chin and pulled the trigger. Before the man's body hit the floor, Mr. Death had already gunned down two other agents. Mr. Death moved through the smoke filled room when an agent kicked his gun out of his hand and landed a stiff punch to Mr. Death's chin. The blow sent Mr. Death backwards a few steps but he recovered quickly. The agent threw a series of wild punches that Mr. Death blocked easily. Mr. Death grabbed the agent by the arms and smashed his head into the agent's nose shattering it sending blood everywhere. Over the agents shoulder, he spotted another agent trying to creep up on him from behind. He swiftly spun the agent around and removed his back up pistol from the small of his back. Mr. Death used the agent as a human shield as four shots ripped through the agents body. He then raised his arm and put a bullet in the agent's head, his soul leaving his body instantly. Mr. Death made his way through the smoke filled room when two bullets exploded in his chest. The impact from the shots dropped him right where he stood.

# CHAPTER

## 16 DO OR DIE

Angela sat back and watched the pandemonium play out right before her eyes. She watched Mr. Death moved throughout the room like a ghost taking out Secret Service members left and right. She wished the president had listened to her. Angela scrambled over to a dead Secret Service agent and removed his 9mm from his holster. She moved through the smoke filled room with a two handed grip on her weapon. She spotted Mr. Death fighting with an agent and patiently waited for an opening. Once Angela saw an opening, she took it and fired two shots into Mr. Death's chest. Angela then quickly scrambled over to where the president was. She bent down and pulled him up to his feet. "Come on we have to go!" She said leading the president down towards the basement. Angela and the president made it downstairs and the first thing she noticed was the big hole in the floor that seemed to lead down to the sewer. "Come on!" Angela helped the president down into the sewer. The president didn't want to go down into the sewer, but he knew it was either hop down into the sewer or die so he chose the sewer. They made it down into the sewer when he heard a voice call out, "Wait up!"

Angela spun with her gun aimed at the voice, but eased her finger off the trigger when she saw that the voice belonged to Steve. Steve hopped down into the sewer and the trio quickly began making their way as far away from the charity event as possible.

* * *

Mr. Death peeled himself up off the floor. The bullets put a dent in his body armor but for the most part, he was okay. He looked to his left and saw the Teflon Queen and the president headed towards the door that led to the basement. Mr. Death headed towards the basement door when a Secret Service agent charged towards him with a knife in his hand. The Secret Service agent swung the knife with force aiming for the assassin's throat. Mr. Death jerked his head back avoiding the knife strike, in the process he caught the agent's arm in mid-swing and delivered a rib shattering knee to his ribs. The agent howled in pain as Mr. Death violently threw him down to floor and shoved his known knife down into the agent's throat.

Mr. Death stood back to his feet when he felt a strong hand on his shoulder. He quickly spun like a helicopter, breaking the agents hold landing an eight punch combination to the agent's face and chest area until he finally crumbled down to the floor. Over to his left Mr. Death spotted two agents with guns in their hands moving in on him. He quickly dived and came up in an army roll with his gun in his hand. The two agents toppled down face first, both sported tiny holes in the middle of their foreheads. While his back was turned, an agent ran up on Mr. Death from behind and threw him in a choke hold. Mr. Death aimed his gun down at the agent's shoe and pulled the trigger sending a bullet down into his foot. The agent immediately released his grip. Mr.

Death spun out of the agent's grip and shot him in the face. He didn't even stand around to see the agent's body hit the floor; Mr. Death jogged down the basement steps and hopped down into the sewer. He couldn't see Angela or the president, but he could hear their footsteps splashing through the filthy sewer water. Mr. Death immediately took off in a light jog after his prey.

# CHAPTER

## 17 THE ESCAPE PLAN

fter running for ten minutes straight, the president felt as if his legs were going to go out on him. His lungs were on fire and his heart felt like it was ready to jump out of his chest. "Ho... hold up I need to take a rest for a second," the president huffed breathing heavily as he took a knee in the middle of the sewer.

"Come on we have to keep moving," Angela, pressed. Time wasn't on their side and she knew it. She knelt down and helped the president back up to his feet. The president coughed repeatedly as he did his best to keep up with Angela and Steve. The president ran for three more minutes before he finally collapsed down into the grit and sewer water. "I can't make it,"

He announced with his eyes closed.

Steve quickly pulled Angela to the side. "We have to think of something cause the president can't continue," he said with a nervous look on his face.

Angela didn't know what to do. She was used to being the hunter and not the one being hunted. While she stood there thinking she heard the sound of a train rumbling by which told her that they were close to a train station. "Pick him up we have to keep moving or else we're all going to end up dead," she said as she watched Steve pick the president up and toss him over his shoulder like a sack of potatoes and took off in a light jog. All they had to do was make it out of the sewer so Steve could call in for back up and they would be fine or so Angela thought.

Angela and Steve finally made it out of the sewer and onto the train tracks. Up ahead they could see the lights and hear a bunch of chatter letting them know that was the train station platform ahead.

"My radio is working!" Steve announced. "This is special

agent Steve requesting for immediate back up! I have the president with me and we are in danger!" He yelled into his sleeve. By this time, the president had gained a second wind, and was able to jog on his own. They reach the platform and Steve and Angela helped the president off the tracks up onto the platform. Angela then quickly hopped up onto the platform when Steve stumbled into her holding the back of his thigh as blood ran through his fingers. Angela looked over her shoulder and saw Mr. Death quickly approaching.

"Go on without me I'll buy you some time," Steve said pulling his back up 9mm from the small of his back. Angela didn't want to leave Steve behind but now she didn't have no other choice.

"We can't leave Steve," the president said.

"We have to go!" Angela said as she pushed the president along through the thick New York City crowd.

Steve spun around and aimed his gun in Mr. Death's direction, but the assassin was no longer there. Steve quickly raised his gun up in the air and sent two shots into the ceiling. He knew the sound of the shots would send the thick crowd into a frenzy and maybe give Angela and the president a better chance at getting away.

Out of nowhere, Steve felt his legs get swept from under him. His back hit floor hard as a knife was jammed down into his throat. Mr. Death didn't even wait for him to die before he took off after the president.

\* \* \*

Angela and the president moved through the crowd at a good speed until a young uniform cop stood in front of them with his gun pointed at Angela.

"Let go of the president!" The cop yelled with a firm grip on his gun.

"She's with me!" The president yelled. "Someone is trying to kill us!" He tried to warn the young cop, but it was as if he ignored every word that the president said and kept his focus on the woman with the gun in her hand. Knowing time wasn't on her side; Angela dropped her gun, spun around, and put her hands on top of her head. The cop slowly inched his way towards Angela, reaching out in an attempt to grab her wrist and handcuff her. Angela spun and cracked the young cop in the face with an elbow, in the same quick motion she slapped the back of his hand causing the gun to go off. The bullet hit the floor close to the president's feet. She then grabbed the gun and twisted slightly, dislodging the barrel of the gun from the stock. Angela chopped the young cop in the throat, then viciously stomped the back of the cop's leg dropping him to one knee. She then grabbed the cop's head with both hands in a firm grip and gave it a hard twist. The president looked on as the body of the lifeless cop crashed face first down to the pavement.

"Come on we have to go," Angela grabbed the president by the arm and rushed him along. They reached the top of the steps where several cops awaited the president's arrival. Two cops quickly escorted the president and Angela into a bullet proof truck. Once the president's butt hit the seat, the truck took off. Angela looked back and watched twenty officers rush down the subway steps in an attempt to catch the gunman.

* * *

Mr. Death stepped off the escalator and spotted several police officers rounding the corner. In a flash, his raised his gun and put down five officer's with all head shots. He ducked down as return fire pinged loudly off the escalator. Mr. Death grabbed an innocent bystander, a middle aged woman by the neck, using her as a human shield. He hid behind the woman as he picked off police officer's left and right. Mr. Death peeked around the corner and spotted several officer's moving in on him. He quickly slammed a fresh clip in the base of his gun and laid down flat on the escalator steps, the electric steps automatic sending him down downwards. Mr. Death laid on the escalator steps going down backwards. The first officer tried to hop on the escalator and was rewarded with a bullet to his throat. Mr. Death waved his arm left and right, his bullets cutting through cops like a surgeon. He reached the bottom of the escalator, hopped to his feet and took off in a sprint. Mr. Death sprinted through the train station when out of nowhere he was tackled down to the ground by a Good Samaritan. The big man pinned Mr. Death down to the floor and waited for the cops to arrive. Mr. Death slipped a knife out of one of the compartments in his suit and jammed it in the big man's eye socket then gave the handle a strong twist.

Blood spilled down onto the front of Mr. Death's mask as he kicked the big man off of him. When Mr. Death made it back to his feet, he noticed that the cops had boxed him in, before the cops got close enough to open fire he quickly pulled out a smoke grenade and tossed it down at his feet just as several officers opened fire on him.

"Hold your fire!" The lead officer yelled putting his fist up into the air. When all the smoke cleared him and his team moved in for the kill but Mr. Death was no longer there. It was as if he vanished in thin air.

# CHAPTER

## 18 I APOLOGIZE

Angela stepped out the hot bath tub, dried off and walked throughout her suite completely naked. She was happy to finally be a free woman. She decided that she was going to enjoy herself until the next mission presented itself. Angela removed a bottle of wine from the refrigerator, opened it with a cork screw, and poured herself a glass. Captain Spiller had her staying in the best hotel money could buy so she figured she might as well take advantage of the perks. Angela laid on the bed, took a slow sip from her glass as she thought back on her performance. She gave herself a B+. It had been almost eight years since she'd gotten her hands dirty and she held up pretty well in her eyes. Angela had a few bruises and scrapes, but had conditioned herself to think of pain as a mental thing.

Angela laid across the bed relaxing when the cell phone that Captain Spiller had given her rung. She looked down at the phone and the word "unrestricted" flashed across the screen.

"Hello?" She answered.

"Angela?" The voice on the end snapped.

"Yes this is she."

"The president here just wanted to tell you thank you so much for everything, I really appreciate how you went out your way for me."

"Just doing my job sir," Angela replied.

"Hell of a job Angela I know we kind of got off to the wrong foot I just wanted to apologize and tell you thank you, and if there's anything I can ever help you with all you have to do is say the word."

"Thank you sir and likewise," Angela got off the phone and smiled. It wasn't every day that someone could say that they saved the president's life. She smiled and continued to sip her wine. She figured she might as well enjoy her night because it would only be a matter of time before Mr. Death showed his ugly head again.

The next day Angela headed out early to do a little shopping, something she hadn't been able to do for a while, and she had to admit it felt good to be somewhat free again. Angela went in and out of stores buying things on the unlimited card that Captain Spiller had given her for "Emergencies only" after saving the president's life it was only right that she was allowed to shop. Angela racked up on all the things she needed and had been deprived of for the last eight years, but while she shopped she help but to think about Ashley. Angela blamed herself for not being there for, Ashley, she knew Ashley was grown and, more than capable of holding her own but Angela still felt like it was more she could of done to keep her protected. Angela walked past a newspaper stand and purchased a copy.

The front page read "Failed Attempt on the president's life" and under the head line was a picture of the president smiling. Angela smiled knowing her skills were what kept the president alive. Angela looked at the date on the paper and realized that this was the same day eight years ago that she had met Ashley. She remembered it like it was yesterday, she'd never forget the frightened look on the young girls face when she bumped into her in the staircase. Eight years later, Angela would have never thought that, Ashley would become a trained killer that worked for the C.I.A.

Angela grabbed a bouquet of flowers, slipped in the back seat of a cab, and shut her eyes for a minute. Sleeping like a normal person wasn't something she was privileged to do. Angela's mind was always thinking so even when she laid down it was hard for her to fall asleep. Her eyes may have been closed but her ears were working over time listening for anything out of place a habit that she'd picked up years ago. The cab stop at the cemetery. Angela paid the cab driver and slid out the back door. She walked over towards a tombstone where a woman was standing.

"Hey I thought I would find you here," Angela said placing the flowers on the tombstone.

"This was the day my life changed eight years ago," Ashley said staring down at her father's grave. "You know what's crazy?" She asked never taking her eyes off the grave. "That if my father was a regular working man I would have never met you," she laughed as tears rolled down her face. "Sometimes I wonder what my life would of been like if my father would of lived a normal life."

"I hate to say this but people like you and me weren't made to be normal," Angela said softly. "You have a gift I saw it in you when I first met you."

Ashley smiled. "I was just thankful that you saved my life. I owe you."

Angela chuckled. "You don't owe me anything I just did what I felt was right."

"My father may of lived a life of crime, but he was a good man," Ashley wiped the tears from her face. "You know Mr. Death will be coming for us soon right?"

Angela nodded. "I know and I'll be ready when he does," she leaned over and hugged Ashley. "If you need me I'll be in my room," she said leaving to give, Ashley her privacy. Ashley remained at the grave site for a few more minutes to pay her respects, but she couldn't stay there all day, she had to get focused, and get back to work. Ashley knew that, Angela was going to need her help, and she planned to be ready.

# CHAPTER |

## 19 REHABILITATION

The next morning Ashley stepped foot inside the training facility for some much needed work. She wasn't happy with her last performance against Mr. Death and planned on improving her skills, not to mention she needed to test the strength in her newly repaired arm. Over in the corner, Ashley spotted a seasoned agent that went by the name Frank hitting the heavy bag.

"Hey Frank can I get some work?" Ashley asked slipping on a pair of four ounce glove with the fingers cut off, the kind that UFC fighters wear.

"Sure," Frank replied with a smile. "But don't think I'm

going to take it easy on you because you off of an injury."

"Please don't," Ashley smiled as her and Frank stepped in the ring. Ashley put on her head gear, slipped a mouth piece into her mouth, and waited for Frank to do the same. Ashley and Frank met in the center of the ring and touched gloves, then prepared for battle.

Frank set it off by firing a quick jab that snapped Ashley's head back. He knew Ashley was one of the best when it came down to hand to hand combat and really wanted to test out his skills. Frank fired off another quick jab, followed by a sweeping right hook. Ashley slipped the jab easily and ducked just as the hook missed her. The first thing that Ashley wanted to do was test out her arm that had been broken. With the quickness of a rattle snake Ashley fired off a right hook to the head and body. Frank was able to block the hook to the head, but not to the body. The power from the hook caused Frank's entire lower body to shift. Immediately Frank's competitive spirit kicked as he rushed Ashley back into a corner and threw a power left and right to her body then followed up with an uppercut that lifted Ashley's head up. Ashley blocked the body shots and took the upper cut like a champ, during the exchange she was able to slip in a nice counter shot that bounced off the side of Frank's head. Frank stepped in and threw another jab. Ashley slipped the jab, grabbed the back of Frank's head with both hands and delivered a rib shattering knee to his midsection, then followed up with a quick upper cut, hook combination that snapped Frank's head back.

The loud blows and action in the ring had caused everyone in the facility to crowd around the ring to witness a good old fashion fight.

Ashley got on her toes as she began to have her way with, Frank landing al of her shots at will. It had only took Ashley a minute to get back into the swing of thing and get, Frank's timing down. Every time Frank threw a shot, Ashley quickly countered it. The rest of the agents that crowded around the ring "oooh and ahhhh'd" with her every shot that Ashley landed.

Ashley fired a quick double jab that left blood running down Frank's nose; she then followed with a swift kick that bounced off Frank's head gear. Blood and sweat flew from Frank's face and stained a few of the agents that stood around the ring. After that last kick Frank began to get desperate he faked high and went low and scooped Ashley's legs from up under her and dumped her down hard on her back. Frank then threw a series of punches mixed with elbows trying to rearrange, Ashley's face the same way she had rearranged his. In between the punches, Ashley grabbed a hold of one of Frank's arms and applied an arm bar.

"Arrggghh!" Frank screamed as he tapped out. Ashley immediately released Frank's arm when she felt him tap out, stood to her feet, removed her head gear, and gloves.

"Good work," Ashley held out her fist.

"I only let you beat me because I felt sorry for you and didn't want to hurt you," Frank lied as he bumped fist with Ashley.

"Thank you I appreciate it," Ashley said sarcastically. It felt good to beat up on Frank and it helped Ashley's confidence, she knew going up against Mr. Death and Abdul that confidence would play a big part in the entire mission. Ashley showered and then headed back to her hotel room where she planned on resting until the next mission presented itself.

\* \* \*

Captain Spiller sat at the round table along with members

from the Central Intelligence Agency (CIA) and National Security Administration (NSA) at an undisclosed location.

"So I heard one of your people saved the president's life," a woman with blonde hair who represented the CIA spoke.

"You could say that," Captain Spiller replied, taking a sip from his coffee. He hated to have to meet with the CIA and NSA but he needed their approval on a specific matter. "I came here because I have information on Abdul," he paused to take in their reaction. "I got word that Abdul is meeting with the Russian mafia?"

"Meeting with the Russian Mafia for what?" Blonde hair asked.

"I don't know but if I had to guess I'm guessing their meeting to put something big together," Captain Spiller said.

"So what is this meeting all about?" A member of the NSA huffed in an aggravated tone.

"I would like to send one of my agents out to Russia to see what they can capture and maybe even eliminate Abdul," Captain Spiller said. "Abdul already tried to get the president executed I

116

could only imagine what he's planning next."

"What happens if one of your agents is captured then killed on the job?" Blonde hair asked.

"There are no records that none of our agents even exist," Captain Spiller said simply. "They all know the risk of the job."

"I'm in," Blonde hair said. "If this blows up in your face we never had this conversation."

"Understood," Captain Spiller nodded.

# CHAPTER
## 20 DO YOU ACCEPT?

Lieutenant Banks made a pit stop at the liquor store before heading home. The news about what had happened to the president forced him to work overtime. A part of him kind of wished that maybe the president had of been killed that way him and Abdul's business would of finally been over. Lieutenant Banks couldn't wait to go upstairs and have a nice stiff drink. He went to stick his key in the lock when a gloved hand roughly clamped down over his mouth and the cold barrel of a gun was pressed to the side of his head.

"Open the door!" The voice growled. Lieutenant Bank did as he was told, fear taking over his entire body. Once inside the house the gunman spun Lieutenant Banks around and back slapped him down to the floor as if he was a woman. Lieutenant Banks looked up and saw Mr. Death standing over him with his gun aimed at his forehead.

"What do you want from me?" Lieutenant Banks touched his lips and his hand came away bloody.

"The Teflon Queen," Mr. Death spat. "I need to know everything you know about her!"

"I don't know much about her," Lieutenant Banks said honestly. He had yet to even see her in person.

"She works at your company you have twenty four hours to find out as much info as you can on her!" Mr. Death holstered his weapon and made his exit leaving Lieutenant Banks on the floor with a dumb look on his face.

Downstairs Mr. Death hopped in his bullet proof B.M.W and pulled out into traffic like a maniac. For the past three days, all that was his mind was the Teflon Queen. She had to go point blank period. Abdul called Mr. Death once the president hit got botched and told him to abort the mission. Abdul felt that the president got his message loud and clear. Mr. Death's business in the states was over, but he remained. He wasn't leaving the states until the Teflon Queen was in a bag. He could tell from the few run-ins with her that she was the real deal and he looked forward to the challenge.

He parked his B.M.W on the corner, grabbed a bag out of the front seat, and left the hazard lights blinking. Mr. Death smoothly slid down the stairs of the crowded subway station. With so many people down there made it easy for him to blend in. Mr. Death made his way down towards the platform and waited for the next train to arrive. Mr. Death waiting until rush hour to be sure that the train station was packed. When the train arrived, he squeezed inside the cart and held on to a pole. The train was so packed people began to push and squeeze inside the cart. The doors closed and the train began moving heading towards the next stop.

Mr. Death stood in the middle of the cart squished like sardines in a can, but that was alright because what he was about to pull off would be well worth being uncomfortable for a few minutes. When the train slowed down and prepared to stop at the next station, Mr. Death unzipped his bag and looked down inside.

120

Inside the bag were twenty hand grenades, when the train stopped and the doors opened, Mr. Death quickly pulled the pin on one of the grenades and dropped it back inside the bag. He then sat the bag down on the floor and slipped off the train just as the doors were closing. Mr. Death walked off continuing with his night as the train cart that he was just in along with serval other train carts exploded right behind him. Mr. Death casually walked up the stairs and out of the train station as if nothing ever happened. Instead of going after the Teflon Queen, he was going to make her come to him.

* * *

Pow! Pow! Pow! Pow! Pow! Pow! Pow!

"I like this one," Angela said as she stood wide leg working on her aim. Her target was a man made out of card board with a black bandana wrapped around his head. Angela wanted to make sure that she was over prepared for when the next mission presented itself. Angela fired off over five hundred rounds before calling it a day. For the past two and a half weeks, Angela basically lived in the shooting range. She tested out several different guns and the one gun that she fell in love with was the Five-seven hand gun. After a long day of shooting, Angela received a call from Captain Spiller telling her to meet him at the base. From the tone of his voice, Angela could tell that it was time to get back to work.

Angela arrived at the base and smiled when she saw Ashley standing next to Captain Spiller and Troy.

"Glad to have you back soldier," Angela smiled and hugged Ashley.

"Glad to be back," Ashley replied with a smile.

Angela gave Ashley a motherly look, checking to make sure she was all right and all her wounds had healed properly.

"I'm fine," Ashley, told her.

"It's time to get to work ladies!" Captain Spiller barked getting everyone's attention. "Your mission if you choose to accept is to fly out to Russia and get answers from a man named, Brian Zimmerman,"

"Who's Brian Zimmerman?" Angela asked.

"He's the person who's going to lead us to Abdul," Captain

Spiller explained. "Brian Zimmerman is Abdul's right hand man and his accountant, you get to him, and you get to Abdul."

"What's the catch?" Ashley asked. She had been in the business too long to know that, that sounded a little too simple.

"The catch is Abdul is in Russia, but he's flown under the radar, we suspect something big is about to go down we just don't know what," Captain Spiller explained. "Abdul has gone off the radar and now Brian's in charge. Your job is to find Brian and get him to talk by any means necessary."

"What is Abdul and Brian doing in Russia?" Angela asked. None of this was adding up.

"I have no idea but whatever it is I know it's really big,"

Captain Spiller said. "I need you three to go out to Russia capture Brian and get him to talk, Angela you're in charge!" He then turned his focus on Ashley. "Ashley you back her up and Troy I need you to be their tech man, I have a jet with all of y'all gear waiting for y'all already," Captain Spiller smiled. "Now go hunt some terrorist!"

For the first twenty minutes on the jet, Angela paced back

and forth, while Ashley and Troy were looking at the layout of Brian's home on a computer screen. Angela mentally needed to get herself ready for what was to come. Abdul was one of the most deadliest terrorist to ever walk the face of the earth, so mentally she had to prepare herself for all the blood shed that was sure to come. Angela walked over and grabbed her bag. Inside was a fully body armor suit that she stepped into that went underneath her clothes. Two outfits lay at the bottom of her bag, an all-white fatigue suit, and an identical black one. In the weapons department she grabbed a knife, a Five-seven hand gun, several clips, and a FN P90 auto sub machine gun. Covering Angela's face was a ski mask with the entire eye section missing to protect her from the cold. She also grabbed a pair of night vision goggles. Captain Spiller had everything they could possibly need on the jet, now all they had to do was complete the mission.

"Come take a look at this!" Ashely called out. "Two entrances, the front door, and back door, also there will be five guards throughout the property."

"That won't be a problem," Angela said.

"Once you get inside you're going to have to move quick," Ashley told her. "We don't know if Brian has a panic room in his house, if he gets to that panic room he'll have time to call for back up and tip Abdul off that we're there. So under no circumstance is he to reach that panic room,"

"Copy," Angela replied as Ashley went and slipped on her gear. For the rest of the ride the trio remained silent stuck in their own thoughts. When the jet landed, the trio went from the jet to the van that awaited them. The van was full of equipment. Troy got behind the wheel and pulled off like a mad man. After about a thirty minute, drive the van began to slow down.

"Alright ladies get in position, we're pulling up on the Brian's house in two minutes I repeat two minutes!"

Angela looked over at Ashley, "Be careful," she said holding out her fist.

"Always," Ashley replied, bumping fist with her mentor.

"Now!" Troy yelled from behind the wheel.

Ashley opened the back door to the van and jumped out while it was still moving. She hit the ground and rolled, lucky for her the six inches of snow that covered the ground helped break her fall. Ashley army crawled until she could see the front of Brian's house. Her all white fatigue outfit helped her perfectly blend in with the snow. Ashley was roughly a hundred feet away from the front entrance. She quickly pulled out her sniper rifle and peeked through the scope. "I'm in position and it looks like two heavily armed tangos are walking back and forth around the front of the estate."

"We're pulling up to the front gate now," Angela's voice boomed loud and clear through her ear piece.

Through her scope, Ashley saw the white van pull up. She then put her cross hair on the first guard, she pulled the trigger, and he went down. By the time, the second guard realized what was going on his brains popped out the back of his head decorating the white snow. "Both tangos are down!"

"Copy," Angela replied as she crawled out the back of the van and swiftly hopped over the Iron Gate that was built to keep intruders out. In a low crouch, Angela ran through the snow. She reached the door and placed a snake recorder under the front door. She moved the snake around to show her what was on the

126

other side of the door. Once she was sure that the coast was clear, she pulled out a set of lock picks and picked the lock on the front door. Once on the other side of the door Angela pulled out her Five-seven with a snap. She held the fire arm in a two handed grip as she eased her way through the mansion.

"Don't forget there are three more tangos throughout the house somewhere," Troy reminded her as he watched Angela's ever move through the goggles that rested on the top of her head.

Angela eased her way through the mansion when she came across the first guard. He stood with his back turned with an assault rifle in his hands. She aimed her gun at the guard's head and squeezed the trigger. The gun recoiled with a PFFT! Angela quickly ran towards the guard and dramatically slid across the floor on her knees, catching the guard's body before it hit the floor. She then dragged the dead body and dumped it into a storage closet not to draw attention or tip off the other guards. Angela tiptoed her way upstairs and made her way down a dimly lit hallway. She stopped when she heard loud talking coming from one of the rooms. Angela placed her back up against the wall and listened for a second. On a silent count of three, Angela came forward with a strong kick that sent the door flying open. Inside the room, two men sat at table playing cards. Both men had a look in their eyes as if they had just seen a ghost. Angela raised her gun and quickly put both guards down with head shots. "All three tangos are down I repeat all three tangos are down."

Out of nowhere, Angela felt something crash down on the back of her head. The blow caused her to drop down to one knee and lose possession on her weapon. Before she got a chance to gather her thoughts, a pair of strong arms placed her in a deadly choke hold. Apparently, there were six guards in total. The last guard must have slipped by Troy somehow.

The strong guard tried to choke the life out of Angela. She quickly turned delivering a strong elbow to the big man's side before she ran out of oxygen. Then she used all of her strength and flipped him over her shoulder. The guard bounced back up to his feet and took a fighting stance. Angela got on the ball of her feet and landed a stiff jab that snapped the guard's head back. She followed up with a kick to the guard's shin. The flying knee that came next totally caught the guard by surprise, shattering his nose in the process. Angela then finished him off with a strong side kick that sent the guard crashing through the second story window. Angela picked her Five-seven up off the floor and continued towards the master bedroom.

She approached the master bed room and stood still, listening for anything that may inform her on what was awaiting her on the other side of that door. Angela then came forward with a hard kick that sent the master bedroom door flying open. Inside the room, she spotted Brian sitting on his huge bed with a laptop across his lap. "Hands up now!" Angela yelled.

Brian quickly tapped a few more keys on his keyboard before a bullet exploded in his shoulder sending him crashing down to the floor. Angela quickly walked around the bed and picked up the laptop. Whatever Brian was working had been erased.

"Where can I find Abdul?" Angela growled through clenched teeth.

"Go fuck yourself!" Brian said, cleared his throat, and spat in Angela's face. Angela wiped her face, then lifted her leg and stomped Brian's head into the floor repeatedly. She then snatched him up to his feet and shot him in his left foot. "Where's Abdul?"

"I... I... don't know" Brian stuttered. Angela's hand swung in a blur as she back slapped Brian across his face with her gun sending two of his teeth flying. Angela then stomped down on the bullet wound on his feet and applied pressure.

"Ahhhhh!" Brian screamed while Angela had him pinned up against the wall by his throat with her forearm.

"Start talking!" Angela said aiming her gun down at Brian's other foot. Brian looked at Angela as tears ran down his face.

"Please don't do this," he begged.

Angela shook her head, and then fired a bullet down into his other foot. Brian let out another loud scream and tried to collapse but Angela helped him up with her forearm. "Start talking!" She said now aiming her gun at Brian's crotch.

"Okay, okay, okay," Brian, said in a hurried tone. He then yelled out the address to where Abdul could be found.

"Troy did you get that?" Angela asked.

"Got it," Troy replied. "The address checks out and the property is in one of Abdul's girlfriend's name."

Angela turned her focused back on Brian. "What is Abdul

planning?"

"He's planning to send one hundred and four suicide bombers to American," he paused. "Two bombings in each state."

"Why is he doing this?"

"To send a message to your President," Brian said wincing in pain.

"What's the message?"

"To remove all the American troops from places they don't belong!" Brian said. "The American's think they can just do what they want when they want, they go to these poor countries and throw their muscle around. Now Abdul is going to put an end to all that."

"Not on my watch," Angela spat.

Brian laughed. "Abdul has a lot of contacts in America and even more people in his pocket."

"Thanks for the info!" Angela said and then put a bullet in Brian's head. She turned and exited the mansion through the front door. As Angela made her way back to the van, she processed what Brian had just told her. A hundred and four suicide bombers were about to flood the states. Angela climbed in the back of the van and instantly the van pulled off.

"We have to stop Abdul," Ashley said as she reloaded her rifle. She knew if those suicide bombers made it to America, the result wouldn't be pretty.

"We have the address," Troy said from behind the wheel. "It's your call Angela."

Angela paused for a long second. "I think we should head out that way," she figured why sit around waiting for something bad to happen when it was a chance that they would be able to stop whatever Abdul was planning. Two hours later Troy parked the van a half a mile away from Abdul's estate. Angela, Ashley, and Troy all pulled out a pair of heavy duty, night-vision binoculars. "Damn," Angela whispered. Brian's mansion looked like a one bedroom apartment compared to Abdul's estate. The place looked like three high schools all rolled into one.

"I don't like how this looks," Ashley said. Through her binoculars, she saw what looked to be over forty armed guards patrolling the estate.

"I'm going to have to agree with Ashley on this one," Troy said. "We are out muscled and out gunned."

"We have to move now!" Angela told them. "There's no telling what those monsters are in there planning," she paused. "If those bombers make it to the states, we're fucked." Just as the words left her mouth, the trio noticed a limousine pull up directly in front of the mansion. Seconds later a man dressed in an expensive black suit stepped out the limousine followed by Lieutenant Banks. Troy and Ashley's mouth hung wide open once they identified the second man as Lieutenant Banks. Troy quickly snapped several pictures of the man in the black suit and Lieutenant Banks as they entered the mansion.

"You sent those to headquarters?" Ashley asked.

"Yea now we have to wait for Captain Spiller's call," Troy answered.

"Let's get our gear on while we wait for this phone call,"

Angela ordered. "If we don't hear nothing from Captain Spiller within fifteen minutes we're going in!"

# CHAPTER

**21** THE MASTER PLAN

Lieutenant Banks stepped foot in the mansion with a smirk on his face. If everything went according to plan he was going to be a rich man after all of the bombings were successful, with all the information he'd been giving to Abdul from working as a spy was sure to pay off lovely. The man next to Lieutenant Banks went by the name Adam Thomas. Adam's job was to get the hundred and four bombs into the states without any problem. Abdul was paying good money for this operation to be flawless.

Two armed guards escorted Lieutenant Banks and Adam to the sitting area where Abdul sat having a drink while two sexy naked women did a seductive dance for his entertainment.

"Gentlemen," he greeted. "So glad you could join me," he said with a smile. With a snap of his fingers, he dismissed the two naked ladies. "Now let's get down to business, how's everything looking?"

"Everything is all set up and ready to go," Adam said in a convincing tone. "Just waiting on you."

Abdul then turned his gaze on Lieutenant Banks. "Any problems I need to know about?"

"No sir," Lieutenant Banks said with a smile. "Everyone is still shaken up about the attempt on the president's life."

"Perfect," Abdul knew that while the world was still stuck on the attempted assassination on the president's life, no one would be expecting a follow up attack which is the reason why the bombings were perfect. A great time to catch America with their pants down. "What about this Teflon Queen chick I keep hearing about does it look like she's going to be a problem?"

Lieutenant Banks chuckled. "No the last I heard she was one of the agents that's guarding the president right now, so the coast is clear America is never going to know what hit them,"

"Excellent," Abdul smiled. "You both will be paid once the mission is complete I have my men working on getting all of the bombs and explosives packed away now they should be done within the next hour," he told them. "In the meantime let's all have a drink," Abdul snapped his fingers and a butler seemed to appear out of nowhere carrying a tray with three glasses on it.

"To a job well done," Abdul laughed as the three men all clinked glasses.

# CHAPTER

## 22 MISSION IMPOSSIBLE

Angela hung up the phone with a serious look on her face. "Captain Spiller said our mission is to eliminate Abdul, and the man in the black suit."

"What about Lieutenant Banks?" Ashley asked.

"Captain Spiller said he wants Banks alive," Angela said with a smirk.

"Let's get into position!" Angela ordered.

"Angela," Ashley called out. "Please be careful in there we don't know how many of them are in there."

"I'll be fine," Angela held out her fist. Ashley flashed a quick smile before bumping fist with her mentor.

"Your best bet will be to try and go unseen for as long as you can, the last thing you want is a gun fight with an entire army," Troy explained.

"Copy."

Ashley crawled on her stomach through the snow until she reached her position. Once in position she removed her sniper rifle from her back pack. "In position."

"Copy," Angela replied. She ran through the snow in a low crouch until she reached the Iron Gate. She waited a second until the coast was clear before she hopped the gate and landed flat down onto her stomach in the snow. Her all white army suit helped her blend in perfectly with the six inches of snow that covered the ground. When the guard walked past she crawled on her stomach a few feet then stopped when another appeared out of nowhere. "Ashley there's a guard standing directly in front of the entrance can you take him out from where you are?"

"I sure can," Ashley replied. She had the guard's head in the middle of her crosshair, her finger rested on the trigger waiting for the word.

Angela quickly hopped up off the ground and took off in a sprint towards the entrance. "Take the shot!" she yelled.

When the guard noticed a figure in all white coming towards him, he raised his gun but before he got a chance to do anything, his head exploded. Angela then quickly ran up, grabbed the guard's dead body, and dragged it over behind the bushes. She then made her way over to the front door, just as she attempted to pick the lock the door suddenly swung open and out stepped a guard holding a machine gun in his hand. Angela moved in a blur, she staggered the guard with a quick elbow strike to the head, then slipped behind him and threw the guard in a choke hold. The guard tried to put up a fight until Angela ended the battle by snapping his neck. She then tossed his body on top of the other guard's dead body over in the bushes.

"I was able to break into all of the security cameras in the mansion," Troy's voice echoed off in Angela's ear.

"And what do you see?"

"Looks to be around one hundred to a hundred and fifty guards inside the property," Troy told her. "I think we may need to think this over."

"No time for that," Angela said as she entered mansion and tip toes across the marbled floor over behind a statue. "Troy I'm going to need you to be my eyes while I'm in here."

"Copy."

Angela moved quickly down the hallway and placed her back up against the wall. "How many on the other side of this wall?"

"Three tangos heavily armed. They seem to be watching something on a laptop," Troy informed her. "Porn if I had to guess."

"Copy," Angela pulled out her Five-seven with the silencer attached to the barrel, took a deep breath, then sprang from behind the wall, and fired three shots. Angela moved pass the men before they're bodies hit the floor. Angela ran through the dining room area, slid across the floor, and hid behind the counter just as another guard was entering the dining room area.

"You have to take that guard out before he spots the other dead guards," Troy said.

"Copy," Angela removed a hunting knife from her utility belt and crept up on the guard from behind. She slipped a gloved hand over the guard's mouth, jammed the knife in the side of his neck, and gave the handle a strong twist. She then dragged his body and tossed it in the pile with the rest of the dead guard's.

"What's on the other side of that door?"

"Five armed tangos," Troy replied.

"Copy," Angela removed her Five-seven and inched her way towards the door. She took a deep breath then charged through the door. The first guard's head exploded before he even know what hit him. The second guard was stuck as a deer caught in the head lights when a bullet entered his eye and exited out the back of his head. The third guard fell down face first as a small hole rested in the middle of his forehead. The fourth and fifth guard went to reach for their weapons but they weren't quick enough. All five guards were down in three seconds flat.

"Good shooting," Troy said as he watched Angela murder the guard's in cold blood through the security cameras. He had to admit she was the best he had seen so far, and was happy that she was now on his team.

Angela let the clip fall from the base of her gun and replaced it with a fresh twenty round clip. "Thanks," she replied as she began to drag the guard's dead bodies over into a corner instead of leaving the bodies in plain sight. Angela grabbed the last dead guard's legs and started to drag his body when another guard entered the den out of nowhere. She quickly dropped the dead man's legs and whipped out her Five-seven with the quickness of a snake, aimed, and fired. The bullet hit the guard in the center of his throat. The guard gurgled on his own blood before he collapsed down to the floor, but before the guard hit the floor, he managed to get off a shot that hit Angela in the pit of her stomach. The impact from the shot forced her to take a knee. "Shit!" She cursed. It had been years since she'd been shot so the pain was at an all-time high. Her body needed to get used to pain.

"Sorry Angela I didn't even see that guy are you alright?" She heard Troy's voice in her ear piece.

"I'm good my vest stopped the bullet from going through," Angela said climbing back up to her feet.

"You've got company," Troy announced. "The shot that the guard fired must have alerted the rest of the guard's.

"How many?"

"Fifteen!" Troy replied. "You have to get out of there you have around ten seconds!"

Angela quickly ran out of the den and hid down behind a circular water fountain that spit up water in a spray every few seconds. The fifteen guard's walked on the other side of the water fountain and entered the den trying to find out if that was indeed a gun shot or not.

"Okay the coast is clear move!"

Angela ran in a low crouch into another section of the mansion. The mansion was so big it was like running through a maze.

* * *

A guard entered the den and spotted one of his fellow comrades lying dead on the floor in a pool of his own blood. He then looked over and spotted five dead guards laying in a pile over in the corner. The guard immediately hopped on his radio. "We have an intruder on the property it's time to go hunting."

# CHAPTER

**23** STAY ALIVE

Ashley laid flat on her stomach in the snow looking through her scope when she noticed five pickup trucks filled with soldiers holding assault rifles pull up to the front of the estate. "Angela you have to get out of there!"

"My cover has been blown! I'm going to have to shoot my way out of this!" Angela's voice echoed through Ashley's ear piece.

"Shit!" Ashley whispered as she focused on the target in her crosshair. She pulled the trigger and watched the soldier's body crumble down to the ground with a gaping hole in the middle of his forehead. The rest of soldiers looked around frantically for the shooter but came up empty. Seconds later four more soldiers dropped, followed by three more. Immediately all the soldiers rushed towards the entrance of the mansion knowing that, the sniper wouldn't be able to shoot all of them.

Ashley picked off as many soldier's as she could before there were no more targets left. Out of fifty soldiers, around twenty four of them were able to slip inside the mansion. The other twenty six soldiers lay sprawled across the ground with bullet holes inside of them. "Looks like twenty five to thirty soldiers were able to get inside the mansion."

"Copy."

# CHAPTER

**24** OUTGUNNED

Angela tip toed through the mansion when she came across three soldiers. She quickly raised her Five-seven dropping the three soldiers before they even knew what hit them. Before Angela could take another step forward, another soldier popped out of one of the many bedrooms and threw her in a choke hold. Angela quickly lowered her gun and fired a shot into the soldier's leg; she then reached behind her head and flipped him over her shoulder, hopped up and put a bullet in his head. Another soldier mysteriously appeared out of another bedroom just as several other soldiers appeared at the end of the hallway. Angela landed an open hand chop to the soldier's throat, grabbed the hand that he held his sub machine gun in, twisted his wrist forcing him to release his grip on the fire arm. Angela caught the machine gun before it hit the floor, slipped behind the soldier, and opened fire on the rest of the soldier's. She made sure to sure the man as a human shield. The machine gun rattled in her hand as she watched several soldier's hit the floor. Once the coast was, clear Angela continued down the hallway when the sound of a bedroom door opening caught her attention. She spun around and found herself looking down the barrel of a shot gun.

Kaboom!

The impact from the shot gun blast sent Angela flying backwards through a closed bedroom door.

"Arghhh!" Angela groaned as she rolled around on the floor in agony. The shot gun pellets didn't penetrate Angela's armored suit, but it left her with a few cracked ribs and bruises. It felt like she had been hit by a truck. Angela looked up and saw twenty soldier's standing over her with assault rifles trained down on her.

The head guard roughly snatched Angela up to her feet by her hair and tied her hands behind her back with plastic hand ties.

147

Once Angela's hands were tied behind her back, the head guard then stripped her of all of her clothes. Angela stood completely nude with her hands tied behind her back, when the head guard pulled out a .357 magnum and pistol whipped Angela inches away from her life.

The guard beat Angela to a bloody pulp, and then dragged her throughout the mansion by her ankles as if she was an animal leaving a long blood trail behind.

# CHAPTER

**25** SO YOU CALL YOURSELF
THE QUEEN

Abdul and Lieutenant Banks stood enjoying a drink when a gang of soldiers drug Angela inside the room.

"So this is the so called Teflon Queen?" Abdul chuckled. He stood over Angela, raised his foot, and stomped her face down into the floor repeatedly. He didn't like the fact that she had made it so close to him and was so close to shutting down his operation. "Get her up!" He ordered. Immediately two soldiers violently pulled Angela to her feet by her hair, then forcefully sat her down in a steal chair where two other soldier quickly duct taped her ankles together.

"How much do you know about me?" Abdul asked. Angela looked up at him with a straight face and didn't say a word. Her face was a bloody mess and one of her eyes were completely shut. "Did the president send you?"

"She's never going to talk," Lieutenant Banks said. "She's been trained not to talk."

"I have ways to make her talk," Abdul smiled. "And I have all day."

Immediately the legs of the chair were swept from under Angela and she went crashing backwards down to the floor abruptly. Her face was immediately covered with a towel. Two soldiers held each side of the towel while another soldier stood over her with a water hose.

Abdul nodded his head and the soldier let loose with the water hose. Angela gagged and coughed when the towel was blasted with water. She was squirming so much that another soldier had to hold her mid-section down. After hosing her down for twenty five seconds the soldier cut the water, waited ten seconds, then blasted the water again. Again, Angela gagged, couched, and bucked her mid-section like a wild bull.

Abdul raised a hand and immediately the soldier cut off the water hose. He walked over and squatted down beside Angela, snatched the towel off her face. "You have something to tell me?"

"Go fuck yourself!" Angela spat as the towel was forced back over her face and soldier turned the hose back on. Abdul paced back and forth while his soldiers damn near drowned Angela. He knew it was going to be hard to get Angela to talk so he figured he'd have to use a more violent method of torture.

"That's enough!" Abdul called out. "Sit her back up!"

Two soldiers lifted Angela's chair back into the upright position and watched as she gasped for air. Angela was thankful that, that was over but she knew Abdul wasn't letting her off the hook that easy.

"Have something you want to tell me?" Abdul asked as a soldier handed him a blow torch. "How many more are with you?"

Angela said nothing.

"Still not ready to talk?"

151

Angela said nothing.

Abdul turned the blow torch on and aimed it towards Angela's stomach.

"Arrgggghh!" Angela roared as she felt her flesh burning from the heat from the blow torch.

"We going to see if you are really made out of Teflon," Abdul smiled as he turned and back slapped Angela across her face. "Still don't have nothing to tell me?"

Angela said nothing.

"Okay have it your way!" Abdul said as he moved the blow torch down towards Angela's legs. Angela shut her eyes as the pain ripped through her entire body. The heat from the blow torch had her feeling as if she was in hell. "Please...please!"

"Please what?" Abdul yelled. "Now you want to talk?" he turned and slapped Angela across her face. "What do you have to tell me?"

"Pl... pl... please turn up the temperature, I'm freezing in here," Angela flashed a bloody smile. She knew she was going to die so she figured why not go out with her self-respect.

# CHAPTER

**26** TIME TO GO TO WORK

Ashley laid flat on her stomach in the snow when she heard several different machine guns being fired all at the same time through her ear piece. "Angela you there? Angela? Angela?" She called out but got no answer. Ashley listened carefully and was able to make out a few noises that sounded like a wounded animal moaning and groaning. "I'm going in there to get her!"

"You can't!" Troy said quickly. "There's too many of them!"

"I'm not going to sit here and just let her die!" Ashley quickly pulled out an FN P-90 sub machine gun and attached a silencer to the barrel. "Can you break into the electric system from your computer?"

"Of course I can," Troy replied.

"Great be on standby," Ashley said as she ran towards the entrance in a low crouch. She entered the mansion and immediately spotted the bodies of several dead soldiers. Ashley moved throughout the mansion like a ghost until she came across two soldiers standing making small talk. She quickly raised her FN P90, put the two soldiers down, and was gone before their bodies even hit the floor. The further Ashley moved through the mansion, she could hear the sound of a woman screaming at the top of her lungs. She could only imagine what those sick fucks were doing to her. A soldier turned the corner catching Ashley off guard. She swiftly spun and jammed a knife in the middle of the man's throat and eased him down to the floor. Ashley removed the knife from the man's neck when two more soldiers appeared out of nowhere. Without warning Ashley tossed the knife like a dart at the first soldier, she watched as it flipped through the air finding a home in the soldier's eye. Ashely then did a front flip roll, came up, and put a bullet in the second soldier's head.

"Good shooting," she heard Troy's voice through her ear piece. Ashley moved throughout the mansion when she saw movement from the corner of her eye. A room door opened and a big soldier appeared. Before Ashley got a chance to do anything, the big man snatched her inside the room. The big man held Ashley from behind in a bear hug type of grip and tried to squeeze the life out of her. Ashley could feel the big man's grip sucking the life out of her. She quickly lifted her legs and pushed off the wall with all her strength sending the big man crashing back into a huge portrait that covered the wall. The big man's head bounced off the wall forcing him to release his grip. Ashley made it to her feet first and unloaded a series of punches and elbows to the big man's head. The big man took the punches well as he grabbed Ashley, lifted her up over his head, and then forcefully brought her down across his knee.

"Arggghh!" Ashley howled. Before she could get up off the floor, she felt the big man's boot in the pit of her stomach. Ashley crawled back to her feet just as the big man was throwing a powerful haymaker. Ashley caught the big man's arm in midair, and then took him down to the floor in an arm bar. She applied pressure to the man's arm until the sound of his bone snapping could be heard followed by a loud pain filled scream. She then crawled on top of him, grabbed his neck, and gave it a deadly twist. Ashley made it back to her feet just as two more soldiers entered the room. Ashley spun and landed a spinning back elbow to the side of the first soldier's head. She watched as the man's head violently bounced off the wall, before his body hit the floor she was on to the next soldier. The soldier threw a wild hook that Ashley ducked easily and came up with a knee to his gut followed by a back hand closed fist. Another soldier must have heard all the commotion from the hallway and came charging into the room. He spotted Ashley and immediately threw two hooks with bad intentions. He watched as Ashley weaved his two punches before his feet got swept from under him. He hit the floor hard and before he could sit up Ashley jammed a knife in the middle of his face. She then repeated the gesture repeatedly until she was sure that the man was dead.

Ashley stepped out into the hallway where another soldier stood waiting for her. He landed a stiff right cross that violently snapped Ashley's head back. He tried to follow up with another

156

punch when Ashley slice his hand with the knife, then jammed the blade into his solar plexus. When the coast was finally clear Ashley picked up one of the soldier's assault rifles from off the floor and continued towards the sounds of a person screaming. She made her way through the mansion, and then stopped suddenly when she could hear screams along with several other voices coming from the next room. Ashely crept alongside the wall and peeked her head around the corner. Inside the room, she saw Angela sitting strapped down to a chair while Abdul held a blow torch to her skin. Around twenty to thirty soldiers stood around enjoying the show.

"Troy are you there?"

"I'm here," Troy replied in less than a second.

"I got twenty to thirty tangos in the room along with the package," Ashley whispered as she slid her night vision goggles down over her face. "In five seconds I need you to cut the power to the entire house."

"Copy," Troy said. "And Angela still has her ear piece in her ear so she can hear you."

Troy's voice reverberated in Ashley's ear.

"I'm coming in to get you Angela!" Ashley said just as all the lights in the house went out turning the entire place pitch black. She grabbed a grenade, pulled the pin, then reached around the open door, and dropped it in. The soldier's shouted in alarm, followed by a tremendous explosion that caused the entire building to shake. Ashley quickly spun around the corner with a firm two handed grip on her assault rifle. All of the soldier's that were still standing were illuminated in a green glow making it easy for Ashley to find her targets. The gun rattled in her hands as she watched several soldiers drop like flies while the rest of them scattered not wanting to get hit with one of the assassin's bullets. The bullets from the assault rifle chopped down as many soldiers as they could until there were no more soldiers left standing.

"Troy cut the lights back on!" Ashley said as she kneeled down behind Angela's chair and cut her loose. She looked down at Angela's wounds and winced. "You okay?"

"I'm fine," Angela replied as she snatched the Five-seven from Ashley's holster. Seconds later the lights came back on.

158

"Come on we have to find Abdul before he tries to escape."

"You need medical attention."

"I'll be fine," Angela spat as she headed in the last direction she saw Abdul headed. Her mind was so focused on killing Abdul that she totally forgot that she was naked. Angela and Ashley headed down to the basement area where they spotted Abdul and Lieutenant Banks trying to escape out of a back door.

"Don't move!" Angela shouted. Abdul went to reach for the door when a bullet exploded through the palm of his hand forcing him to drop down to a knee.

Ashley looked around and noticed several huge metal crates lying around. She grabbed a crowbar that laid next to one of the boxes and broke into one of the boxes. Inside the box was full of explosives. "Shit these are all the explosives that he was going to send to the states," she said to Troy as she began snapping pictures of all of the boxes.

Abdul looked up at Angela from the floor. "Name your price."

"Fuck you!" Angela spat, pulled the trigger, and watched

159

Abdul's head violently jerk back. She then walked over to make sure that Abdul was dead when out of nowhere Lieutenant Banks reached in the inside of his blazer. Angela quickly moved her gun from Abdul to Lieutenant Banks but before she got a chance to pull the trigger she witnessed his head explode, as his lifeless body then crumbled down to the floor. She looked over at Ashley who held a smoking gun, and gave her a wink.

"Ladies it looks like you've got company," Troy announced as he saw several army trucks full of soldiers pull up in front of the mansion on his computer screen.

"How much time do we have?" Angela said as her and Ashley rushed upstairs.

"Three minutes tops!"

"Copy!"

Angela and Ashley rushed through the mansion until they made it out the back door that led to a balcony type of deck. The two women looked down, it wasn't a long jump, but it wasn't jumping over a puddle either. Angela and Ashley leaped off the roof, landing in a snow bank. Angela dropped, rolled, and came up unharmed; she immediately felt a chill run down her spine as her bare feet sunk down into the snow. She was trained to be able to withstand pain, but the cold weather was something totally different. She spotted two soldiers over to her right and quickly put them down face first into the snow. Angela was in a tremendous amount of pain, but her inner strength and survival skills urged her to keep pushing. Up ahead Angela spotted three snow mobiles parked next to a pickup truck. Before she could reach the snow mobiles a soldier, riding a snow mobile appeared out of nowhere heading straight for her and Ashley. Angela saw him reaching for a gun, but before he got a chance to reach it she delivered a spinning heel kick to the soldier's head knocking him clean off the snow mobile. The move hurt Angela's already wounded body badly, she then hopped on the snow mobile and fired it up as she felt Ashley slip on behind her and grab a hold of her waist.

"Hold on!" Angela yelled over her shoulder as the snow mobile took off at a high speed. She hadn't drove one in years but it seemed to all be coming back to her rather quickly.

"You guys got some company!" Troy announced. Angela

looked over her shoulder and spotted several soldiers on snow mobiles on their trail.

"Shit!" Angela cursed. "Hey give me your night vision goggles!"

Ashley quickly removed the goggles from her head, slipped them over Angela's head, and fixed them over her eyes, making sure she could see. Angela switched the night vision goggles on and cut the headlights off on the snow mobile. She then turned off the road and headed into a thick forest, zigzagging through the trees at a high speed. Angela zoomed through the dark forest as the heat from bullets sliced through the air near her head. A few bullets hit the back of the snow mobile and caused Angela to lose control.

WHAM!

The snow mobile grazed a tree, then the last thing Angela remembered was her and Ashley being tossed into the air. Her body rotated midair for a few seconds before landing hard on the ground. They both were thankful that they didn't hit a tree or a sharp rock. Angela and Ashley's body hit the ground and their momentum violently forced them down a deep hill. Their bodies

162

tumbled for what felt like five minutes straight before finally coming to a stop.

When Angela's body finally came to a stop, she sat and looked around for Ashley. "Ashley! Ashley!"

"I'm right here," a voice said causing Angela to turn around. Angela spun around and her face lit up when she saw Ashley limping towards her with a smile on her face. The two hugged one another tightly. They were both just happy to be alive. Seconds later, a van came to a screeching stop in front of the two women.

"Come on we have to go!" Troy yelled from behind the wheel. He pulled off just as Ashley and Angela hopped in the back of the van. Several bullets pinged and ricocheted off the back of the van until it disappeared into the night.

# CHAPTER

**27** GLAD TO BE HOME

Angela, Ashley, and Troy stepped off the jet and were immediately met by Captain Spiller.

"Great job!" Captain Spiller said in a stern tone. "You three are heroes!"

"I tried to bring Lieutenant Banks back alive but I wasn't able to work that out," Angela spoke.

"It's okay I'm just happy you all made it back in one piece," Captain Spiller said. "You three single handedly saved our country."

"Well sir it was a team effort and I wouldn't have been able to do it without these three by my side," Angela replied.

"Job well done," Captain Spiller said cracking a smile for the first time. He then escorted Angela over to the awaiting ambulance. Her appearance told him that she was in severe pain.

Ashley walked over while the paramedics were putting Angela in the back of the ambulance. "You alright?"

Angela smiled. "Did you forget I'm made out of Teflon," the two shared a good laugh. "Thank you for saving my life back there that was real brave of you."

"As many times as you saved my life I figured I owed you," Ashley held out her fist.

Angela bumped fist with Ashley as the paramedic closed the door to the ambulance and pulled off. Angela laid on the stretcher in the ambulance and just reflected on everything she had been through. It wasn't that long ago that she was sitting in a jail cell thinking she would never see her freedom again, now only months later here she was saving the president's life as well as the rest of the country. Angela laid on the stretcher staring up at the ceiling, the last thing she remembered was one of the

165

machines beeping, then one of the paramedics placing a mask over her face just as she faded out.

\* \* \*

Two days later, Angela woke up in a hospital bed with several tubes and wires plugged into several different machines. She looked over to her left and spotted Ashley sitting in a chair next to her bed sound asleep. The site of Ashley next to her bed sleep brought a huge smile to Angela's face. She could tell that Ashley genuinely had love and cared for her. Angela took a moment and just stared at Ashley taking in everything. She remembered the scary little girl that she met in the mall years ago, and to see her now sleeping in the chair brought a tear to her eye. Angela was proud of how far Ashley came, not to mention how good of an agent she had become. "Wake up sleepy head," Angela sang.

Ashley stirred, opened her eyes, and smiled. "You're awake!" She said excitedly.

"How long have I been here?"

"Two days," Ashley answered. "They gave you some medicine that put you out so your body could get some much

166

needed rest."

Angela smiled. "Thanks again for saving my life."

Ashley waved her off. "You would have done it for me; besides we are heroes now."

"Did the media have a field day with the Abdul story?"

Ashley shook her head. "They ran it into the ground; it's been on every station for the last two days."

"Well at least Abdul is dead and this is all over," Angela breathed a sigh of relief.

"I think we make a good team," Ashley said. "Thank you so much for always being there for me. When my parents died the only person I had in my corner was you, and I want to say thanks for never turning your back on me."

"Come here," Angela pulled Ashley in close for a hug. "We're family now and we'll always be family."

"Pinky promise?"

Angela smiled. "Pinky promise."

"Now that I know that you're alright I can run home and take a shower," Ashley stood to her feet.

"You coming back?"

"I'll be back within two hours tops," Ashley leaned over and kissed Angela on the forehead. "Get you some rest."

"Okay I guess I'll take another nap be careful out there," Angela said as she watched Ashley exit her room.

Ashley stepped foot outside of the room and nodded towards the three agents that stood down the hall making sure that no one was allowed in Angela's room, except for the nurses and doctors. "Don't let nothing happen to my girl."

"Don't worry she's in good hands," one of the agents said as he watched Ashley disappear in the staircase.

# CHAPTER

**28** END ALL BE ALL

Mr. Death pulled up in front of the hospital and killed the engine. He had paid top dollar to find out which hospital the so called Teflon Queen was residing in. He had become obsessed with tracking down and killing Angela and today would be the perfect time. He stepped out the vehicle, entered the hospital, and walked straight up to the front desk. "I need the list of names of every one of your patients and what room they're in."

The blonde hair woman that sat behind the desk looked up at the man that stood in front of her as if he was insane. "I'm sorry sir but I'm not allowed to do that, it's against the law and I could lose my job."

Mr. Death pulled out a machine gun in a blink of an eye and blew the woman's brains out in front of everyone. After the shot was fired, several screams could be heard followed by the sound of people stampeding over one another trying to get out of the hospital. Mr. Death hopped over the counter and clicked a few keys on the keyboard and instantly the entire list of every patient that resided in the hospital appeared on the computer screen. Mr. Death looked closely at the screen and saw that the patients on the fifth floor were unlisted and there was no information found anywhere. That let him know that Angela was somewhere on the fifth floor.

Mr. Death hopped back over the counter and was immediately confronted by two security guards. He quickly gunned down the two security guards and made his way over towards the elevators. As Mr. Death waited for the elevator, he saw a group of employees trying to sneak by him headed towards the exit. He aimed his machine gun in their direction and squeezed down on the trigger until there was no one left standing.

170

Mr. Death boarded the elevator, pressed five, and watched as the doors closed, he stuck a fresh clip in his machine gun and waited patiently for the doors to open. The elevator doors opened with a loud ding. Mr. Death saw several nurses and doctors waiting to board the elevator. Without warning Mr. Death raised the machine gun and chopped down several employees, he then stepped off the elevator and put a bullet in one of the agent's head, then quickly took cover behind the counter as the remaining two agents returned fire. Mr. Death pulled a flash grenade from his belt line, pulled the pin, and then tossed the grenade over his shoulder. He waited for the blast before he sprung from behind the wall and quickly gunned down the two remaining agents. Mr. Death stepped over the agent's dead body and entered the first room down the long hallway. He stepped in the room and saw two older men lying in separate beds with nervously looks on their faces. Mr. Death raised his gun and filled both men with bullet holes. He then stepped out the room and made his way towards the next room, he wasn't leaving the hospital until the Teflon Queen was dead, and he didn't care if he had to check every room one by one.

# CHAPTER

**29** SURVIVED

Angela laid in the bed sleep when she was rudely awaking by the sound of bullets followed by loud pain filled screams. She sat straight up, snatched all the wires and tubes from her body, and slid out the bed bare foot. Angela didn't know what was going on, but she knew she wasn't going to stick around to find out. Angela stepped out into the hallway and could hear the gun shots only a few doors down. She ran down the hallway as fast as she could and tried to slip into another room undetected but when several bullet holes decorated the wall just above her head she knew immediately that she had failed. "Shit!"

Angela cursed loudly. There she was trapped in a room, with no gun and nowhere to go. "Think, think, think," she said looking around the room for anything she could use as a weapon. Angela's eyes scanned the room and stopped when they made contact with a pencil lying on top of a clip board. She quickly ran over, grabbed the pencil, and held it in a firm grip, placed her back up against the wall, and waited for the drama that she knew was surely to come.

* * *

Ashley stepped out the staircase and stopped in mid stride. She looked around and saw several dead bodies lying all over the place, instantly she pulled her Five-seven from her holster and headed straight for the elevator when out of nowhere she heard a loud blast that shook the floor. Immediately she knew that Angela was in trouble, Ashley knew, Angela was in no condition to properly defend or protect herself. She then quickly hopped on the elevator and pressed five.

* * *

Mr. Death slowly made his way towards the room that he saw

173

Angela enter. He placed a fresh clip in his gun, stood in front of the door and squeezed down on the trigger, while waving his arms back and forth. The gun rattled in his hands as he watched the bullets cut through the door and walls. When the gun was empty, Mr. Death stuck another fresh clip in the base of his gun just to unload it through the door and walls again. The wall and door resembled a slice of Swiss cheese. Mr. Death placed a fresh clip in the machine gun, and then came straight forward with a strong kick that sent the door flying off the hinges. Mr. Death cautiously entered the room, he took two steps inside when out of nowhere Angela jammed a pencil in his hand, and then grabbed his machine gun with two hands. The gun fired repeatedly as the two struggled and fought over the gun.

BRRAT! TAT! TAT! TAT! TAT! TAT!

Once the gun was empty, Mr. Death released his grip from the gun and delivered a sharp upper cut to Angela's stomach. The impact from the blow caused Angela to double over in pain. Mr. Death then took a step back and kicked Angela in the face as if he was kicking a field goal. Blood spilled from Angela's mouth and painted the wall.

Angela quickly got herself together, stood, and took a fighting position. She took a step forward and fired a jab. Mr. Death easily slipped the jab and landed a bruising hook that rattled Angela's rib cage. Angela took the punch well and countered with a sneaky over hand right that landed on the side of Mr. Death's face. Angela then faked high, but went low trying to deliver a powerful kick to Mr. Death's ribs, but he was ready for the kick and caught her leg. With her leg in his grip, Mr. Death went to twist her ankle and break it, but Angela was prepared for the maneuver. She quickly rotated her body in the same direction as the twist, her hands hit the floor, and at the same time, she sludge hammer kicked Mr. Death in the abdomen with her free foot causing him to release her leg. Angela charged Mr. Death rushing him back into the wall. With his back against the wall, Mr. Death's blocked all the body blows that Angela attempted to deliver and fired a hard knee to Angela's chest. She took the knee like a champ and caught his leg in the process, lifting him off his feet and slamming him down on his head. Mr. Death quickly made it back to his feet and fired off a quick one, two. The first shot violently snapped Angela's head back, but she

175

caught the second punch and tried to place Mr. Death's arm in an arm bar, but like a veteran, he easily blocked the attempt.

Mr. Death slowly walked up to Angela and hit her with an eight punch combination, followed by a spinning heel kick that bounced off the side of Angela's head. The impact from the kick sent her crashing over top of the bed on to the other side of the floor. Angela slowly crawled back up to her feet, when she felt dizzy, and weak that last kick to the head made it seem as if everything was spinning. Mr. Death walked up and fired off a kick to the side of Angela's leg, her ribs, and then her head all in one fluid motion. His leg never hitting the floor. Angela looked up from the floor amazed by his foot speed and accuracy. She was injured and knew there was no way her skills could match his in her current condition but still she crawled back to her feet. Angela's ego and pride refused to let her stay down. Angela threw a weak punch that had little chances of landing. Mr. Death caught Angela's arm and hip tossed her over his hip. He held Angela's arm up and stomped down on it where the forearm and elbow connected.

CRACK!

"Arrgggggggghhh!" Angela howled like a wounded animal as she felt the bone in her arm snap like a branch.

Mr. Death slowly walked up to Angela and stood over her. "Pay back is a bitch!" He growled, raised his leg, placed his foot on Angela throat, and applied pressure. Angela struggled to get his foot off her neck with her one good arm but it was no use. She could slowly feel the life escaping from her body in small breaths.

Mr. Death smiled as he watched Angela's eyes begin to roll in the back of her head. He went to apply even more pressure when Ashley appeared in the door way and put four bullets in his chest dropping him right where he stood.

Bang! Bang! Bang! Bang!

Ashley inched towards Mr. Death's body when out of nowhere with the quickness of an alley cat he sat up and tossed a throwing knife at her face. Ashley leaned back as far as she could trying to avoid the knife but it still managed to somehow lodge into her shoulder. Mr. Death leaned back on his shoulders and popped back up on his feet and ran full speed towards Ashley; he hit her hard, lifted her off her feet, and rammed her back into the wall. The momentum caused them to both go crashing through the wall and into the next room.

# CHAPTER
**30** BACKUP

Captain Spiller pulled up to the hospital and worked his way through and the police and media. The front of the hospital looked like a zoo with people floating around the property. The cops did their best to get pedestrians to back up and not cross the police tape. Captain Spiller stood getting briefed by an officer when he heard someone call his name. He spun around and saw a man in S.W.A.T gear standing in front of him. "Can I help you?" Captain Spiller asked in an aggressive tone.

"I'm Sergeant Baker, and I'm in control now!" He said with

authority. "Me and my team are going in."

"Wait you can't I have two of my agents in that hospital,"

Captain Spiller told him.

"Sorry but I received specific instructions from the president himself!" Sergeant Baker announced.

"What instructions?"

"My instructions were to terminate every last living thing in that building," Sergeant Baker said. "It's said to believe that there's a terrorist in there and of course you know we don't negotiate with terrorist."

"Fuck a terrorist two of my agents are in that building god damn it!" Captain Spiller barked.

"May God be with them sir!" Sergeant Baker said then returned over to the S.W.A.T truck.

"Son of a bitch!" Captain Spiller cursed as he watched what looked to be around twenty S.W.A.T team members enter the hospital. The part that pissed him off the most was that there was nothing he could do to stop them. "I hope Angela and Ashley are as good as they say they are."

# CHAPTER

**31** STAYING ALIVE

Angela slowly crawled back up to her feet, looked out the door, and saw Ashley and Mr. Death over in the room across the hall both fighting for their lives. Without thinking twice, she ran out over to the other room and joined the action. While Ashley held Mr. Death's attention, Angel landed a sneaky punch to his kidneys followed by a kick to the ribs. Mr. Death turned and readied to punch Angela's head off when suddenly his feet were swept from up under him. He hit the floor hard but bounced back up to his feet as if nothing happened. Angela and Ashley attacked Mr. Death at the same time. Fists flew from every direction, Mr. Death blocked most of the blows while backing up, his arms, and hands were moving at an all-time high speed.

Ashley charged Mr. Death and tried to scoop his legs from up under him, while holding on to his waist. Ashley pulled the knife that was clipped to her belt and jammed it down into Mr. Death's leg. Meanwhile, Angela landed a flying kick that violently snapped Mr. Death's head back and sent him crashing out into the hallway. Angela and Ashley quickly followed Mr. Death out into the hallway. Ashley rushed, Mr. Death back into the wall, but he quickly used her momentum against her, and slammed her into the wall instead. As if he had eyes in the back of his head, he stopped Angela from creeping up on him from behind with a swift kick to the face that stopped her dead in her tracks. All three assassins took a fighting stance, backing down or bowing out was a thought that never crossed any of their minds. Angela inched towards Mr. Death when the staircase door busted open and two grenades rolled towards their feet.

"Shit!" Angela's eyes lit up as all three of them took off, diving in the air as the explosion helped spring board their bodies even further. Mr. Death's body violently hit the wall and then fell down to the floor. He quickly made it back to his feet when he saw, Three S.W.A.T members quickly run over in his direction. Once the S.W.A.T. team saw the assassin make it back up to his feet, they opened fire. Mr. Death smoothly disappeared in the staircase as the S.W.A.T bullets ripped through the staircase door and walls. He laid on the floor and removed his back up .380 from his ankle holster. The first S.W.A.T team member that entered the staircase was rewarded with a bullet to the throat. The next S.W.A.T member tossed a smoke grenade in the staircase. When the blast erupted the remaining two S.W.A.T members entered the staircase and opened fire, they didn't have a target hoping that one of their bullets would find a home in the assassin's body. The two S.W.A.T members eased down the steps when the sound of footsteps coming from behind them startled them. Before they could even turn around, Mr. Death jammed a knife down into one of their necks, and then shot the other one in the face.

Mr. Death quickly moved down to the next floor, when he heard footsteps from up above. He wasn't sure how many

183

S.W.A.T. Members were in the building, but he knew had to get them before they got him. Mr. Death ran down the stairs skipping two at a time, when out of nowhere the staircase door came busting open and two S.W.A.T. Members eased through the door. Before the S.W.A.T. Members knew what had hit them. Mr. Death jumped down a flight of stairs and landed a flying kick that took the first S.W.A.T. Member off his feet, the second S.W.A.T. Member turned his rifle on the assassin. Mr. Death hands moved in a blur, he landed open hand chopped the S.W.A.T. Member's throat, then swept his feet from up under him before he had a chance to even grab his throat. Mr. Death stood over the wounded S.W.A.T. Member's body and fired a bullet into his face. Just as the gun went off, he noticed two other S.W.A.T. Members bust through the same door that the first two had entered through. Mr. Death spun with the reflexes of a cat and dropped the first S.W.A.T. Member; he then turned his gun on the next S.W.A.T. Member and pulled the trigger. He watched as the bullet bounced off the S.W.A.T. guy's helmet. The S.W.A.T. guy hit the floor, raised his rifle, and opened fire on the assassin. The bullets from the M-16 rifle spun Mr. Death around

184

like a windmill sending him violently crashing down the stairs.

The S.W.A.T. guy slowly stood to his feet and spoke into his earpiece. "Shots fired on the third floor, suspect is down!" He slowly eased his way down the stairs, then stopped dead in his tracks when he saw the assassin sit up with a gun in his hand. Before he even got a chance to do anything, a bullet ripped through his Adam's apple and exited out the back of his neck.

Mr. Death watched the S.W.A.T. guy's lifeless body tumble awkwardly down the stairs landing directly next to him. "Fuck!" Mr. Death cursed as he slowly peeled himself off the floor, stumbled down to the second floor, and exited the staircase. The M-16 bullets didn't penetrate through his skin but the impact and force from the shots had really damaged Mr. Death internally. From experience, he could tell that he had a few broken ribs and maybe a punctured lung. Mr. Death used the wall to help hold him up as he spit out blood. He quickly duck inside of a patient's room when he heard soft footsteps coming from up ahead.

Mr. Death looked down at his hand gun and noticed that it was empty. With each breath he took felt as if his organs were about to collapse at any giving second. When the footsteps

185

became loud enough that he could pin point where the person was, Mr. Death sprang from out of the room and landed a blinding quick kick to the side of an S.W.A.T. guy's head, the force from the kick knocking the helmet straight off the man's head. Before the S.W.A.T. guy got a chance to recover, Mr. Death followed up with a four punch combination to the man's face. Out of natural reflexes the S.W.A.T. Threw a lucky and powerful hook that landed directly on Mr. Death's rib cage. The punch folded Mr. Death like a paper bag.

"Get your ass up!" The S.W.A.T. Member growled as he roughly snatched the assassin up to his feet then roughly slammed the man's head into the wall repeatedly. He then dug his fingers in Mr. Death's eyes and tried to rip them out of the socket.

Mr. Death dropped down into a split and landed a powerful uppercut to the S.W.A.T. guy's groin area causing him to drop down to his knee. In a quick motion, Mr. Death removed a small knife from his utility belt and jammed it in the S.W.A.T. guy's throat.

Mr. Death slowly made it back to his feet when he heard a

door bust open from behind him; he quickly spun around, looked down, and saw a grenade rolling towards his feet. "Shit!"

* * *

Ashley crept up on one of the S.W.A.T team members from behind, stomped down on the back of his leg, forcing him to drop down to one knee. She then snapped his neck before he got a chance to fight back. She then grabbed the dead man's body and dragged it back into the room that she had just come out of. "The only way we going to make it out of here alive is to put on one of these S.W.A.T uniforms," she said looking over at Angela. "Here you take this uniform and I'll take the next one."

Angela quickly stripped the dead man down and put on his uniform. She then took the dead man's helmet and put it on that way she wouldn't be recognized. Angela grabbed the dead man's machine gun and tossed it to Ashley. She then grabbed his back up hand gun and exited the room. Immediately Angela ran into four S.W.A.T members. She took a knee as if she was injured and as soon as the other members got close to her to see if she was all right, she fired off four shots. All neck shots. Angela dragged one of the dead men bodies back to the room where Ashley waited. Ashley quickly jumped into the S.W.A.T uniform.

"Come on let's get out of here," Angela said as her and Ashley walked through the hallway as the sound of an intense gun fight rang out loudly on the floor above them. They immediately knew that Mr. Death wasn't going out without a fight.

"I hope they kill him," Ashley said as her and Angela boarded the elevator.

* * *

Captain Spiller stood outside in front of the hospital with a nervous and concerned look on his face, until he heard someone yell. "We got two coming out!" Captain Spiller watched the two S.W.A.T members exit the hospital. He smiled when the S.W.A.T members removed their helmets and long hair flowed down their backs. "Wait! Don't shoot!" Captain Spiller yelled as he ran towards Ashley and Angela and hugged them both at the same time. He didn't care if they were injured or had blood on them; all that mattered to him was that they were both still alive. "We need a medic over here immediately!" He yelled. Instantly a team of paramedics surrounded Angela and Ashley and tended to their needs.

While the paramedics were looking at Angela's arm, Captain Spiller walked over. "So is the dead?"

"I'm not sure, the last time I saw him he was still alive," Angela answered honestly.

"Well they just sent forty officers in there so hopefully they'll be able to kill that bastard," Captain Spiller informed her.

Forty minutes later Angela heard someone yell. "We've got a survivor!" Immediately she turned and saw an S.W.A.T team member being helped out of the hospital. She yelled over and got Captain Spiller's attention. "Did they find his body yet?"

Captain Spiller shook his head with a defeated look on his face. "No sign of his body anywhere, all the bodies they found belong to either patients, staff, or S.W.A.T."

"Impossible he's got to be in that building somewhere," Angela fumed.

"Don't worry we'll catch him next time, don't beat yourself up over this," Captain Spiller patted Angela on the back. Just as Angela was about to lose hope she noticed something. She looked over at the final survivor and something about him just wasn't right. The survivor walked with a bad limp and seemed to be in server pain. "Captain you got a gun on you?"

"Of course I do why?"

"Give it to me!" Angela stood to her feet, grabbed the gun, and headed over towards the wounded survivor. Angela slowly walked over to the survivor with the gun hanging down by her side. She wasn't sure about what she was doing, but she had to make sure. "Remove your helmet!" she demanded when she reached the survivor.

"Ma'am this man needs medical attention. I'm going to have to ask you to step back!" one of the paramedics barked.

Without warning, Angela slapped the paramedic across the face with the gun knocking her unconscious. "I said take your fucking helmet off!" Angela yelled aiming her gun at the man's head drawing the attention of everyone.

The survivor slowly removed his helmet and on the other side of the mask stood Mr. Death. He flashed a bloody smiled at

Angela. "I'll see you in hell."

"Indeed!" Angela said, and then blew Mr. Death brains all over the side walk. Angela dropped the walk and slowly walked back over towards Captain Spiller and Ashley.

"Good work Angela," Captain Spiller said with a huge smile.

"How'd you know it was him?" Ashley asked.

"His limp, I remembered you stabbed him in the leg while we were fighting." Angela pointed out.

"So what's next for the Teflon Queen?" Ashley asked.

"Rest," Angela chuckled. "I need to rest and maybe even a vacation."

"I was talking about as far as the job goes."

"Well I don't know that depends on my partner," Angela flashed a smile. Ashley returned her smile and hugged her tightly.

"You got two months to get all the rest you want," Captain Spiller, said raining on Angela's parade.

191

"I could definitely use two months off," Ashley smiled.

"I was talking to Angela not you, Ashley," Captain Spiller joked.

"Hey you heard my partner we need to rest call us when the next mission presents itself," Ashley smiled as her and Angela walked off.

"Oh don't worry I'm sure I'll be calling you both real soon," Captain Spiller laughed as he watched his two new favorite agents walk off. "Job well done ladies… Job well done…"

*To be continued . . . .*

## Trivia Question

What is Abdul Ockbar's best friend/accountant name?

1. Email to g2g@good2gopublishing.com with the correct answer to the trivia question.

2. With your trivia answer attach a screen shot or paste a copy of your review to verify your purchase along with your name asap.

3. Both must be received by Feb 22nd11:59PM

The $300 Fan Giveaway winners will be announced Feb 23rd on a Facebook Post and in the Feb 23rd email blast.

## New Release Free

Good2go Publishing Presents - Flipping Numbers PT 1 by Ernest Morris

**New Release**

48 Hours To Die: An Anthony Stone Novel by

Silk White

**Free E-Books From Good2go Publishing**

**Limited Time Only**

*The Serial Cheater PT 1 By Silk White*

*He Loves Me, He Loves You Not By Mychea*

*Tears Of A Hustler PT 1 By Silk White*

*Slumped PT 1 By Jason Brent*

*My Boyfriend's Wife PT 1 By Mychea*

The Panty Ripper PT 1 By Reality Way E-Book

# Books by Good2Go Authors on Our Bookshelf

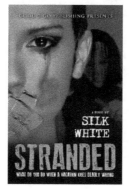

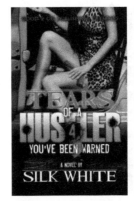

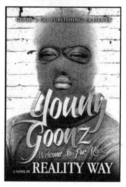

## Good2Go Films Presents

*To order books, please fill out the order form below:*
*To order films please go to* www.good2gofilms.com

Name: _____

Address: _____

City: _____ State: _____ Zip Code: _____

Phone: _____

Email: _____

Method of Payment:     Check     VISA     MASTERCARD

Credit Card#: _____

Name as it appears on card: _____

Signature: _____

| Item Name | Price | Qty | Amount |
|---|---|---|---|
| 48 Hours to Die – Silk White | $14.99 | | |
| Flipping Numbers – Ernest Morris | $14.99 | | |
| He Loves Me, He Loves You Not - Mychea | $14.99 | | |
| He Loves Me, He Loves You Not 2 - Mychea | $14.99 | | |
| He Loves Me, He Loves You Not 3 - Mychea | $14.99 | | |
| Married To Da Streets – Silk White | $14.99 | | |
| My Boyfriend's Wife - Mychea | $14.99 | | |
| Never Be The Same – Silk White | $14.99 | | |
| Stranded – Silk White | $14.99 | | |
| Slumped – Jason Brent | $14.99 | | |
| Tears of a Hustler - Silk White | $14.99 | | |
| Tears of a Hustler 2 - Silk White | $14.99 | | |
| Tears of a Hustler 3 - Silk White | $14.99 | | |
| Tears of a Hustler 4- Silk White | $14.99 | | |
| Tears of a Hustler 5 – Silk White | $14.99 | | |
| Tears of a Hustler 6 – Silk White | $14.99 | | |
| The Panty Ripper - Reality Way | $14.99 | | |
| The Teflon Queen – Silk White | $14.99 | | |
| The Teflon Queen 2 – Silk White | $14.99 | | |
| The Teflon Queen – 3 – Silk White | $14.99 | | |
| The Teflon Queen 4 – Silk White | $14.99 | | |
| Time Is Money - Silk White | $14.99 | | |
| Young Goonz – Reality Way | $14.99 | | |
| | | | |
| Subtotal: | | | |
| Tax: | | | |
| Shipping (Free) U.S. Media Mail: | | | |
| Total: | | | |

**Make Checks Payable To:  Good2Go Publishing - 7311 W Glass Lane, Laveen, AZ 85339**

CPSIA information can be obtained
at www.ICGtesting.com
Printed in the USA
LVHW050919190219
608010LV00016B/250